THE CRAFT OF BEING COVERT

THE SIDEKICK'S SURVIVAL GUIDE MYSTERIES, BOOK 6

CHRISTY BARRITT

River Heights

CHAPTER ONE

"NOW THAT SCHOOL'S officially out for the summer, my parents are taking Chloe on a trip to the mountains for the week." Michael Straley's warm voice floated through the phone.

I shoved my cell between my ear and shoulder as I reached into my purse for my keys. "A trip to the mountains sounds like fun."

Despite my lighthearted words, my back muscles tightened. The darkness around me felt more ominous than usual, and the sidewalk where I stood was barren. If it hadn't been an emergency, I wouldn't be out here right now. But our receptionist Velma had insisted I needed to stop by the office tonight.

"The good news is . . ." Michael's voice softened,

almost as if he was telling me a secret. "I thought maybe I could take you on an actual date."

I shoved my key into the lock of the Driscoll and Associates office building and twisted it. My heart lifted at the possibility of spending some alone time with Michael. It could be just what our new relationship needed.

"That sounds really nice," I told him.

"True fact. Let me do some planning, and I'll get back with you. Anyway, I've got to go help Chloe pack right now. Where did you say you are?"

"Velma texted me." I shoved my keys back into my purse, task completed. "She said she left a file on my desk that I needed to look at tonight."

"Since when does Velma leave work stuff for you after hours?" Surprise stretched through Michael's voice.

"I thought the request was strange also. But Velma hasn't quite been herself lately. It's really no problem for me to stop by and check it out."

Two weeks ago, Velma had been abducted by the Beltway Killer. Since being rescued, she'd thrown herself back into work, but I still worried about her mental state. Dealing with a serial killer wasn't exactly the type of ordeal a person got over quickly.

"Be safe, Elliot," Michael said. "I'll see you tomorrow."

Warmth filled me when I heard the tenderness in his tone. I was pretty sure Michael liked me just as much as I liked him. That thought made me very happy.

"Good night, Michael," I murmured.

I slipped inside the dark office building and twisted the lock in place behind me. I couldn't afford to be careless, not given everything that had happened lately. The past several weeks had been filled with doozies.

Who was I kidding?

The past several months had been enough to knock me over and call me a bridge. It was a Yerbian expression —Yerbian meaning being from Yerba, a small South American country. My family and I had just moved from there to Storm River, Virginia, at the beginning of the year, and I preferred my country's colorful expressions to most of the Americanisms I'd been puzzling over for the past several months.

I stepped from the entryway into the reception area. As I did, I reached for the light switch.

I flipped it up, but nothing happened.

Weird. Was there some type of power outage in the area?

I pictured myself on the sidewalk. The other buildings close to our office had definitely had lights on. I remembered wondering if the baker two doors down was working late catering an event. Their storefront had been lit up like a tree fern filled with fireflies.

So what was going on with this office?

Maybe just this room was out of power.

With a sigh, I found the flashlight on my phone and used the beam to guide me through the reception area and into my office. I'd grab the folder Velma had left for me and get out of here.

I wasn't afraid of the dark, but knowing how effortlessly it could conceal things made me nervous—especially after everything that had happened as of late. My life had flashed before my eyes on more than one occasion.

As I stepped into the office I shared with Michael, I glanced at my desk.

The space appeared just as I'd left it. Everything was in place. Organized. Skillfully arranged, if I did say so myself.

But there was no folder on my desk.

I frowned.

Before I could double-check the text Velma had sent me less than an hour ago, a noise across the room caught my attention.

My heart pounded in my ears.

Had that been a footfall?

Gripping my phone, I swung the flashlight toward the sound.

The beam flickered across the room, catching dust particles floating in the air.

I sucked in a breath when I saw something in the corner.

A man.

Wearing a mask.

A chicken mask.

CHAPTER TWO

"WHO ARE YOU, and what are you doing here?" I stepped away, the back of my knees hitting the desk chair. I nearly fell into it, but I caught myself in time.

The figure stepped toward me. "You mean, you do not already know that answer, Elliot Ransom? I always took you for a smart girl. Too smart for your own good."

The man's sultry, teasing voice had a distinct Spanish accent.

I had no doubt the man behind the mask was from Yerba. Long story short, my father had been a spy there, and, ever since he died, I'd sensed someone watching me.

In some ways, I'd been anticipating this moment—minus the chicken costume.

But I clearly hadn't been anticipating this enough.

If I had truly known this would happen, I would have been more prepared.

My throat tightened until I could hardly breathe.

I needed something to defend myself with.

I only had my phone.

And maybe the stapler in my desk drawer if I could grab it in time.

Which I knew I couldn't.

I stared at the intruder. At the beady eyes on his costume. The colorful feathers. The orange beak.

"I don't have any information." A tremble captured my voice. "The jump drive was stolen before I could crack the code and get into it. But you know that, don't you?"

"You are valuable to us, Elliot." The man's voice sounded entirely too calm and only proved to chill my blood even more. The mask made him appear even more eerie, more imposing.

Especially since I had no idea what his face looked like behind it.

I shouldn't be afraid of a bird. But I knew what I'd just heard. I had to be tough, even when the going got rough. If not, I might—

I couldn't even keep rhyming, my natural go-to when I felt fearful. It was a technique my father had taught me. Instead of dwelling on fear, I turned my thoughts to something I could control—like coming up with amateur poetry.

But I had no time for that. Right now, all my energy needed to be on survival.

"What do you mean, 'I'm valuable to you?'" My heart pounded into my rib cage with enough force that an ache formed.

I really had no idea what Chicken Man was talking about. If I had useful information, I would have used it by now. Didn't these people know that?

Chicken Man stepped closer, his feet seeming to glide across the floor. "If you do not get the intel to us, there will be consequences. Serious consequences."

"I can't get you something I don't have." What was he talking about when he said consequences? Was he threatening me?

I didn't want to think about it.

The man moved even closer. "I am certain that you do not want to find out what we will do if you do not hand it over."

"I promise, I don't have anything." My voice trembled. "Leave me alone."

"Oh, *señorita* . . . if only that was possible. Consider yourself warned."

The man raised his hand. Before I could react, a spray hit my face.

I coughed as panic flooded me.

I tried to back up, to run—but failed.

Everything blurred around me.

I sank to the floor.

Whatever was in that spray . . . it must have contained a sedative.

Before I could fight back, blackness consumed me.

CHAPTER THREE

MY EYES JERKED OPEN, and I stared at the blackness around me.

Where was I, and how had I gotten here?

A few seconds later, the dark office came into focus.

I was still at Driscoll and Associates.

Panic stretched through me as a memory of what happened flooded back.

My gaze jerked around the room.

Was the intruder still here?

My gut told me no, but I needed to be certain.

Carefully, I climbed to my feet. I wobbled a moment as I tried to find my balance.

When my head stopped spinning, I glanced around.

My brain didn't register any movement in the office.

No sound.

I glanced at the front door. A streetlight illuminated it, and I noted the lever was vertical.

It was unlocked.

Most likely, that meant Chicken Man had fled in that direction.

I expelled a deep breath, trying to get my racing heart under control.

That man could have killed me.

But he didn't. The only reason I was still alive was probably because he thought I had intel that he was desperate to get.

But I had no idea what that information was.

My hands trembled as I grabbed my phone from the floor, where I'd dropped it. I dialed Michael's number, hardly able to breathe as I waited for him to pick up.

"You just couldn't wait any longer to talk to me, could you?" He answered on the first ring, a teasing edge to his voice.

I wished this call was playful, but it wasn't. "Michael, I'm at Driscoll and Associates. An intruder was inside."

"What? Are you okay?" All the teasing left his voice.

I quickly took an inventory of myself. "I think I'm fine. Just shaken."

"Let me take Chloe to my parents, then I can come out—"

"There's no need." I ran a hand over my shirt, trying to iron out wrinkles—or, more likely, to gather myself. My head still felt woozy, but I was certain it would pass. I just needed to focus. "The man is gone."

Michael paused for a moment. "Did he say anything? Take anything?"

"I don't think he took anything." I hesitated before sharing the next detail. "I . . . know this is going to sound crazy, but he was dressed like a . . . like a . . . chicken."

"A chicken?" Michael said the words as if he was unsure if he'd heard correctly.

"Yes, he was dressed like . . . he might be if he participated in the Festival of the Chicken back in Yerba."

The Festival of the Chicken was an annual Yerbian tradition. The celebration had seemed normal when I lived in South America. People dressed like chickens, wearing feathers and crazy costumes. They danced. They ate poultry cooked hundreds of different ways. Then there were the contests the community held—contests where people pecked like chickens and walked like chickens and ate like chickens.

Honestly, the annual event had been a blast, and I had so many good memories.

But that man had worn the costume into this office not only to conceal his face, but to remind me of what was at stake.

My home country had imploded. My family had gotten out in time. But my father must have known something that could bring the new regime down.

That theory was the only thing that made sense.

"Elliot, just let me come out and meet you—" Michael's voice cut through my thoughts.

"No, really." My gaze scanned everything around me again, but, in my gut, I knew this man was gone. "I'm okay. He just came to scare me. If he wanted to kill me, he would have."

"I don't like the sound of that."

"Believe me, I don't either." Reality tried to squeeze at me, but I pushed it away. "That's a true fact, for sure."

"I'm going to stay on the phone with you as you walk out to your car." Michael's voice left no room for argument.

I wasn't complaining. I could use someone to watch my back right now.

"Okay," I conceded. "I'll grab my keys and go outside."

"We should call the police."

"If I call the police then I have to explain the details about my past—and my dad's past. That means they'll probably talk to my mom to verify details. And, if they do that, I'm going to have to explain to her everything I've discovered."

My mom didn't yet know that my father had been a spy. When I'd learned the information, I'd kept the details to myself—mostly because my mom was dealing with enough stress. She'd already lost the love of her life, taken on two part-time jobs, and she was trying to stay on top of the double lung transplant my teenage sister needed for her cystic fibrosis.

"Okay, we can figure out the police situation later," Michael said. "I just need to know that you're going to get out to your car safely right now."

I gripped my keys more tightly as I stepped toward the door.

Despite the fact that I knew this man had most likely left, that didn't stop the fear from rushing through me. Wasn't that what this intruder wanted? To shake me up? To leave me feeling off balance?

I didn't want him to win.

Slowly, I walked through the space, keeping my eyes and ears open for anything suspicious.

Nothing.

Finally, I reached the outside door. I shoved it open and nearly stumbled onto the dark sidewalk of the quaint street where our office was located.

Once again, I glanced around.

The streets were empty.

I fumbled with the lock until it clicked in place.

"Elliot?" Worry lined Michael's voice.

"I'm here. I'm fine. I'm outside, and I don't see anyone." My words came out fast and more terse than I intended.

"Just be on guard."

"I will be." I slowly crept around the corner to where I'd parked my car in the lot behind the building.

Just ten minutes earlier, swinging by the office had seemed so innocent. But knowing what I did now, all of this seemed like a bad idea. I should have just parked on the street so I wouldn't have to walk back here out of sight from any passersby.

But it was too late to change that now.

Still gripping my keys, I picked up my pace as I hurried across the smooth cement sidewalk. I didn't want to move so quickly that I got careless. But I couldn't move so slowly that I made myself an easy target either.

Finally, my silver Buick with the red door came into view. I rushed toward it, feeling like a horse running toward home.

Just then, something jumped in front of me, and I swallowed a scream.

A cat, I realized.

I placed a hand over my heart.

Just a cat.

"Talk to me, Elliot," Michael's voice came through the line. "Everything still okay? What's going on?"

"Everything's good. It was just a cat. I'm almost at my car."

I reached my vehicle and slid my key into the lock. A moment later, I was inside with the doors locked. As an afterthought, I checked the backseat.

It was clear.

"I'm safe." My shoulders slumped with relief, and I tried to even out my breathing. "I'm going to head home now."

"Are you sure you don't want me to come over?" Michael asked.

I *did* want him to come over. That's what I wanted more than anything—for Michael to be by my side and help me figure this out.

But he had other priorities. Important priorities. Fatherly priorities.

"Stay home with Chloe and get some rest," I told him as I cranked my engine. "We can talk in the morning."

"If you need me for anything . . ."

My heart warmed at the concern in Michael's voice. "I'll call you."

I placed the phone back onto my lap.

Now I just needed to get home in one piece.

I wished that was simply an American hyperbole.

But it wasn't. I honestly hoped I got home without incident.

———

AS I PULLED in front of my house, another wave of relief hit me.

Lights glowed from the windows of the tiny, humble

bungalow. Most people would scoff at the idea of living in such a small, outdated cottage. At least, most people in the wealthy and elite Storm River would. The majority of residents here lived in neighborhoods filled with expensive cars, weekly lawn services, and large lots.

My neighborhood was filled with blue-collar workers.

But this was my safe place, and I couldn't wait to get inside to see my mom and sister.

And then afterward, I couldn't wait to escape to my room to further study the journal my father had left me.

I'd already gone through all the pages more than once. I'd soaked in all the advice my father had left me, even from beyond the grave. Could the information these men were seeking be found within those pages but I just hadn't seen it?

Because they knew I didn't have the jump drive.

What else could that man in the office have been talking about?

I had no idea. But I had to figure it out, and I was going to have to figure it out soon.

After parking, I crossed the cracked sidewalk, went through the chain-link gate, and strode to the front door.

Before I walked into my house, I tried to put on my calmest expression, to conceal any indication that someone had threatened me. I wasn't exactly sure why I tried to protect my mom the way I did. But I did. The last thing I wanted was to add any more stress to her already stressful life.

But sometimes I thought my plan backfired. I thought Mama sensed my anxiety. And I thought that maybe it might even stress her out more to know that I was keeping secrets.

Why were relationships so complicated? No one formula worked for all of them because no two personalities interacted in the same way. I tried to ground each relationship in my life with love and respect, and I prayed those qualities would win out over clashing personalities and differing opinions.

Sometimes—most of the time—it felt like an uphill battle.

I unlocked the front door and stepped inside, where I was instantly greeted by the scent of lavender tea. It was my mom's favorite bedtime drink.

Just as I expected, I spotted her sitting at the kitchen table at the back of the house, with a cup in front of her. When you lived in a small house, you could see from one side to the other. That wasn't always a bad thing. One of my mom's favorite sayings was, "Love grows best in small houses."

As soon as the door opened, Mama climbed to her feet and walked toward me. "Elliot?"

I deposited my purse and keys on the table near the door. "It's me."

Things had felt tense between the two of us lately. We hadn't been seeing eye to eye on various topics for a while. I was hoping that would change now that the Beltway Killer was behind bars, but it was yet to be determined.

"Have you talked to your sister?" She paused in front of me, a wrinkle forming between her eyes.

Instantly, my back muscles tightened. "Ruth? No. I haven't talked to her since this morning. Why?"

"I thought when the door opened it was your sister."

My muscles tightened even more. "Have you tried to call her?"

"I did. Her phone goes right to voice mail."

There had to be a perfectly logical explanation for this. We just needed to think things through. "Did she say she was going anywhere after school?"

Mama stared at me. "She went to one of her friend's houses for dinner. Since I was working tonight, I didn't think it mattered. But I got home about twenty minutes ago and discovered that Ruth still wasn't home."

It didn't sound like Ruth. Sure, she could be irresponsible. But not like this.

At the end of the day, the three of us looked out for each other, in spite of our differences. My sister wouldn't add unnecessary pressure to our already fragile family.

"I'm trying not to worry." My mom smoothed some loose strands of hair from her ponytail away from her face. "I can't find her friend's number, but I'm still looking."

"Let me go look for her. You stay here, in case Ruth comes home. When she does, call me. I'm sure she just lost track of time."

But as I said the words, I wasn't sure at all.

I remembered the man who had broken into my office and the warning he'd given me.

What if he had taken my sister?

My stomach roiled at the thought.

CHAPTER FOUR

I TRIED to tamp down the anxiety that built inside me.

But I couldn't.

I might be naïve in some areas of my life, but I knew better than to think that Ruth's tardiness was something to be easily dismissed.

Yet another part of me wanted to hope that was exactly the case.

My hands gripped the steering wheel as I stared at the dark suburban streets that stretched in neat blocks around me.

I didn't know exactly what I was looking for. I didn't know where Ruth's friends lived. I definitely didn't know where she'd had dinner.

But I couldn't just stay at my house doing nothing.

My phone rang, and I saw it was Michael.

"I thought you were going to call me when you got home." A slight tease rang through his voice. "I've been anxiously waiting by the phone to hear the sound of your lovely voice."

Normally, I might delight in the fact he'd been looking out for me. Not right now, though. "Michael, my sister hasn't come home yet. I'm driving around looking for her."

"What? You don't think this has anything to do with . . ." Worry stretched through his voice, pulling each syllable tight.

I knew what he was going to say. Yerba. My father. That situation.

I wanted to deny it, but I couldn't. "That's what I'm afraid of. I don't know."

"Come pick me up, Elliot." Michael's voice didn't leave room for argument.

"But—"

"No buts about it. I'm taking Chloe to my parents' house, and I'm going to help you look for your sister. Don't try to talk me out of it."

I still wanted to debate with him, but, after a moment of contemplation, I figured there was no use. I had better ways to spend my mental energy.

A few minutes later, I pulled up to Michael's house. He appeared by my driver's side door in five seconds flat and opened it.

He leaned toward me, wearing a "If It Flies, It Spies" T-shirt and his signature baseball hat. The man, with his dark hair and the slight beard framing his face, was handsome, that was certain. I desperately wished I could fully take a moment to appreciate that right now. But I couldn't.

"Why don't you let me drive?" His tone reached beyond the surface and signaled how much he cared.

I looked at my arms, noticing the tremble there. Letting Michael drive was a great idea.

As I stepped out of my car, I expected Michael to climb right behind the wheel. Instead, he pulled me into a warm embrace. I nearly melted in his arms, relishing his strength.

"It's going to be okay, Elliot," he murmured. "We're going to find her."

His words sounded deep and rumbling. Reassuring.

I wanted to believe what he said. I really did.

But my dad was dead, and there was a good chance that the people behind his death were targeting my family.

Knowing that did nothing to comfort me.

"Thank you," I finally choked out, reminding myself to stay positive.

Michael stepped back and planted a quick kiss on my forehead before climbing into the driver's seat. "Let's get going. No time to waste."

I pulled my seatbelt on, and Michael started down the road. My heart pounded with anticipation at what we might discover, at what would unfold over the next few hours. I prayed for good news.

"Where's the last place Ruth was seen?" Michael wasted no time taking the lead.

I welcomed his guidance as panic muddied my own thoughts. "Her friend's house."

"Do you have an address?"

"Let me find out." I should have done that earlier.

I wasn't sure what I'd been thinking. Maybe I *hadn't* been thinking. I'd just been reacting. And that wasn't like me. I was a thinker. Mulling over things was what I did, sometimes to a fault.

As I dialed my mom's number, I desperately hoped when she answered that she'd have an encouraging update. That she'd tell me all our worry had been for nothing.

Instead, her voice still sounded desperate as she asked, "Anything?"

My stomach clenched in disappointment. "Nothing. Not yet. You?"

"No. No one has seen Ruth."

That was what I feared. "What's the name of Ruth's friend she was in a study group with?"

"Lily Marino," Mama said.

"Do you have an address?"

"I don't. I'm not sure where she lives. I just know that the two of them go to school together. I should have—"

"It's okay." I tried to cut her guilt off before it rendered her useless. "I'm going to figure out what her address is. I should be able to find it online."

"Be careful out there, Elliot. I hate to think of you on the streets by yourself right now."

I glanced beside me, gratitude filling me when I realized her words weren't true. "Michael is with me. He's driving right now."

Mom didn't say anything for a moment. "Good. I'm glad you have someone with you. Call me with an update. Please."

I promised her I would.

I only wished I could promise her more.

I wished I could promise her I could deliver Ruth to her door—unharmed, healthy, and happy.

"ACCORDING to what I could find online, that's Lily Marino's house." I nodded to the two-story structure in the distance.

The place appeared upper middle class with its neat yard, clean exterior, and large square footage. The Mercedes in the driveway only confirmed that theory.

Michael slowed the car to a stop in front of it. The

lights were still on inside the house, indicating somebody was probably still awake despite the late hour.

Speaking of which . . .

I glanced at the time.

It was eleven.

I assumed my mom had already called the family, but it couldn't hurt to talk to them again.

Before Michael barely put the car in Park, I opened the door. "Let's go."

I knew Michael understood the seriousness of the situation because he didn't even mess with me. Instead, he climbed out after me and matched my stride as we rushed to the front door.

Before I even knocked, the front door opened, and a woman in her forties stared at us. She was slim with dark, wavy hair that came to her shoulders, and her well-proportioned face held a cultured look.

The woman's muscles went rigid when she saw us. "You must be Ruth's sister."

"I'm Elliot, and this is my friend Michael."

"I'm Andrea Marino, Lily's mom. Lily told me that your mom called."

"Ruth said she was coming over here tonight for dinner," I explained under the glow of the porch light. "Is that correct?"

Andrea nodded. "It is. Ruth probably left here about six thirty. She said she was going to walk home. I offered to drive her, but she said she didn't mind walking."

"She likes to walk places." The habit went back to our Yerbian roots. People walked everywhere in our home country, and driving such short distances seemed wasteful.

"I wish I could help you more." Andrea frowned. "I really do. Hopefully, this is just a misunderstanding, and Ruth will show up at your house soon."

"That's what we're hoping." But my voice cracked as I said the words, seeming to convey my hidden doubt.

Michael's arm shot out and circled my waist, as if he sensed I needed some support right now. He was right.

"Is there any chance we could talk to Lily?" Michael said.

"I've already talked to her, and I'm not sure what else she can tell you." Andrea shrugged, her face still pensive. "But of course you can. Let me go get her."

A moment later, a teen with blonde hair piled in a sloppy bun atop her head appeared.

Lily wasn't the type of person I'd expected my sister to hang out with. The girl looked athletic, maybe even snobby, with her designer shirt and expensive earrings. She hugged her arms over her chest as she stepped onto the porch.

Her gaze went to Michael and me. "Still no word from Ruth?"

"No," I started. "We were just wondering if Ruth said anything about going somewhere else on the way home."

Lily shook her head, her frown deepening. "No, I'm sorry. She didn't. I just assumed Ruth had walked home and crashed for the evening. She was having a rough day —coughing a lot. Do you think she's okay?"

Coughing . . . the reminder only made worry squeeze me harder. So many factors were at play here.

"We're hoping she just got sidetracked," Michael said when I couldn't find my voice. "Has Ruth said anything out of the ordinary lately? Anything that might help us find her?"

Lily shrugged, nothing registering in her gaze.

Until it did.

She shifted and shrugged again, as if trying to forget about whatever thought she'd just had.

"I don't think so." She crossed and uncrossed her arms.

I couldn't let her off the hook that easily. Too much was at stake here. "If there's something you know that might help us find her, you need to tell us, Lily. Please."

"She's right." Andrea turned toward her daughter, her shoulders hunched with tension. "If there's anything you know . . ."

Lily continued to fold and unfold her arms. "Ruth asked me not to tell anybody."

Instantly, my spine straightened. Whatever Lily was about to say wasn't good. I could sense it.

"Lily . . ." Her mom warned again. "Normally, I don't encourage you to share secrets. But in this instance, you need to tell us—especially if Ruth might be in trouble."

After a moment, Lily nodded, though she still looked reluctant.

Finally, she blurted, "Ruth has been talking to someone."

Everything went still around me. "What do you mean?"

"She met some guy online. Sometimes he gives her rides to your house. Well, not right to your house. But he'd drive her to the corner and drop her off so your mom wouldn't see."

My lungs froze.

My sister had met someone online? And then met him in person?

What had Ruth been thinking?

Suddenly, any hopes I had of a good outcome seemed to deflate.

CHAPTER FIVE

AFTER MICHAEL and I climbed back into my car, I let my head fall back against the seat as I tried to digest what I'd just learned. "This is worse than I thought."

He reached over and squeezed my hand. "We're going to find this guy."

I barely heard him. "He could be a predator and have nothing to do with the Chicken Man who confronted me in the office."

Michael studied my expression a moment, his brown eyes steady and reassuring. "Do you really think your sister would run off with some guy?"

I wanted to say no. I wanted to know with my entire heart and soul that Ruth would never do something like this. But I didn't.

"Grief brings about all kinds of changes in people." I

rubbed my throat, hating the fact I had to say these words. "I'm not really sure what my sister might have done. But if she met this guy . . ."

I couldn't even finish the statement. I didn't want to think about the what ifs. I'd seen the news. I knew what often happened in situations like these.

"Let's check in with your mom one more time and then take another trip around the neighborhood. But if we don't see your sister by then, we need to call the police."

I knew Michael's advice was sound.

With one more squeeze to my hand, Michael started the car and began to cruise the neighborhood again. As he did, I kept my eyes open for anyone suspicious, for any sign of what might have happened.

But it was getting late and, at this time of night, there was hardly anybody out.

Though my spirits began to deflate, I called my mom and tried to put on my bravest voice.

Her "hello" came quickly, like the word teetered on the edge of hope and despair. "Anything?"

"We haven't found Ruth," I elected to say. I'd tell her the details about this online man Ruth had met later. "You?"

"No, nothing. Ruth's still not answering her phone. I called a couple more of her friends, but no one has seen her." A soft sob escaped. "I don't like this, Elliot."

"Mama, I'm going to call the police. We need to tell them what's going on."

Another muffled cry sounded on the other end of the line. "You really think so?"

"I do. I'd rather be embarrassed at overreacting than regret not doing everything possible. Michael and I are about ten minutes away from the house. I'll call them and see you soon."

As soon as I ended that call, I dialed the police. Specifically, I dialed Detective Dylan Hunter.

The two of us were friends, and I knew I could trust him. Plus, he knew about my dad so I wasn't going to have to explain that whole situation to him. That should help to expedite the process.

Hunter answered on the second ring, and I told him about my missing sister.

He promised to meet at my house ASAP.

I turned to Michael. "You should go home and be with Chloe before she leaves for her trip."

"I already told her goodbye. They're leaving first thing in the morning."

"But—"

"No buts about it. She's safe and taken care of. I can give all my attention to finding Ruth."

A brief smile brushed my lips. "Thank you."

"Any time, Elliot. Any time."

But as Michael and I drove down my street, my stomach began to churn.

I dreaded to think what this night might hold.

So far, it had been nothing good. And, in my experience, bad things only led to more bad things.

———

I MET Hunter outside my house and explained the situation with my mom to him in private before we went inside. I reminded him that my mom didn't know all the details about my father. I also told him about the man my sister met online and the intruder who'd been in the office.

Hunter promised to use discretion—for as long as possible.

After Hunter took my statement, we sat at the kitchen table with Mom and made a list of Ruth's friends. The police would follow up with each of them.

I would too. As Michael had explained the phrase to me, I would leave no stone unturned.

We'd also given a description of what Ruth had worn this morning. I found a recent picture of her and gave it to Hunter. My mom gave permission to trace Ruth's cell phone signal and check her call log and texts. It all seemed . . . surreal, like something that happened to other people.

"I'm going to need to see her computer." Hunter continued to stare at us from across the table, half friend, half professional.

No, make that *all* friend and *all* professional. He could be both.

The man was reserved but smart. He'd make some woman very happy one day—whenever he decided to open his heart to dating again.

I almost felt like I was experiencing something out-of-body as I walked into Ruth's room, grabbed her laptop, and brought it out.

I opened the screen and typed in Ruth's password.

It didn't work.

"Did Ruth change her password?" I glanced at my mom from across the table.

She looked haggard, as if she'd aged ten years in the blink of an eye. The circles under her eyes were more defined, her skin looked dull, and her gaze appeared empty.

I knew the truth. I knew my family couldn't handle any more tragedy. Losing our home country. Losing the missionary work so important to my mom.

But mostly, losing my dad.

He'd been the rock that grounded us. I would never, ever get used to his absence in my life. And if I did get used to it? Then shame on me.

"Ruth didn't mention to me that she changed her

password." My mom took the computer and moved her hands over the keys. Then she frowned. "I can't get in either."

Without saying anything, we all knew the truth. Ruth had changed the password. She'd broken one of my mother's rules.

The only reason Ruth might do that was because she was hiding something.

Like a secret boyfriend.

Knowing that didn't make me feel any better.

"Any guesses as to what her password might be?" Hunter's gaze volleyed between my mom and me.

I could tell he was treading carefully. Certainly, he understood what we were all going through right now. I appreciated his compassion.

I searched my mind, trying to come up with something my sister might have used for her password. A birthday? The date we'd moved to the States? There were so many possibilities.

"I have a couple of guesses." I reached for the computer. "I just don't want to get locked out."

"Based on what I know about computers, you probably have one more guess," Michael said. "Once you're locked out, you may have to wait an hour or so before trying it again."

"Great," I muttered, feeling more pressure mount between my shoulders.

"If that happens, I'll take it to my guys down at the station and see if they can figure it out," Hunter said. "It's worth a shot."

I knew what Hunter said was true. But I still felt sick, like I might ruin this—ruin our chances of finding Ruth.

Tragedy had exploded, and the aftereffects felt sickly. Reality wanted to set in, but I fought it. I wasn't prepared to deal with the gruesome truth of what I would need to deal with.

I had to believe that we were going to find my sister. I had no other choice right now but to keep that hope alive —because despair would get me nowhere.

I drew in a deep breath before moving my fingers across the keyboard.

My father's birthday. It was my best guess.

I held my breath before I hit the Enter key.

A crash of disappointment hit me.

His birthday hadn't worked—it wasn't her passcode.

The screen remained the same except for the little block of text that popped up, letting me know that I was officially locked out now.

So much for that strategy.

But there had to be a way to figure out what websites my sister had been on.

For now, I turned to Hunter. "What do you need us to do? We can organize people to walk the streets. Make phone calls. I can retrace her steps—"

Hunter raised his hand as if urging me to slow down. "The first forty-eight hours are critical . . . but if Ruth disappeared at six thirty, that means that she's been missing for about six hours. There's still a good chance that she's not actually missing. Maybe she's just being irresponsible."

"She wouldn't do that to us." Mama's eyes gleamed with certainty, and her voice held underlying strains of anger. Not necessarily toward Hunter. But to the situation.

I understood.

Hunter placed a hand on the table, still as calm as ever—which was just what we needed right now.

"Mrs. Ransom, I know that your daughter is a good girl." Hunter leveled his gaze, his voice gentle but direct. "But I don't want to simply believe anything just out of politeness. I need to look at every possibility."

"I just want my daughter back." A tear trailed down the side of my mom's face.

I reached across the table and squeezed her hand. The only thing that made me forget my own grief was thinking about my mom's grief. I would do anything to take the pain from her.

Yet another part of me thought we were acting too hastily. There could still be a reason to believe that Ruth could show up and that nothing was wrong.

"I'm going to call this in so my patrol officers can be

on the lookout," Hunter continued. "We'll also need to check security cameras around the Marinos' house. Maybe we can find some footage of Ruth getting in a car with somebody or something. The best thing that you can do right now is to stay here and monitor your phones. If Ruth comes home, you're going to want to be here for her."

Or if there's a ransom demand. I kept that thought silent.

I leaned forward. "I'm not sure that I can sit still."

"You should be here for your mother." Hunter's gaze locked onto mine. "Let the police do the work this time."

But that was so hard for me to do. I trusted Hunter. I did.

But I was the one with everything at stake right now.

I couldn't lose my sister.

I would do everything I could to find her.

CHAPTER SIX

AN HOUR LATER, a woman from our church—Linda—
arrived to stay with my mom at the house. I'd called her,
knowing Mama shouldn't be alone. However, Michael
and I needed to search the streets more. Calling Linda
had been the only solution I could come up with.

Our efforts would probably be futile. But that didn't
stop me from wanting to do it anyway. Sitting around
doing nothing wasn't an option.

By the time Michael and I finished, we'd driven
around the city for four hours, and the sky was beginning
to brighten as a new day began. As we circled around
another block, Michael turned, as if headed back to my
place.

"What are you doing?" Alarm coursed through me.
He wasn't giving up, was he?

"Elliot, I don't think driving around anymore is going to solve anything." He offered a compassionate frown as he sent me a lingering glance.

I shook my head, knowing I needed to get through to him and make him understand the urgency of the situation. "But maybe it will. Maybe we can still find Ruth—"

"Elliot." Michael pulled to the side of the road and turned toward me. "I know you want to do something. I can only imagine how difficult this is. But we need to use our time and resources in a different way. We've driven around all night, and we haven't found Ruth yet. We need to move forward with another plan of action."

My insides wanted to crack, but I couldn't let that happen. I needed to stay strong. For Ruth. For my mom.

Michael's words made a lot of sense. At this point, the two of us were just wasting time.

He gently ran his fingers through my hair and pushed a few stray locks out of my eyes. "Maybe you should lie down for a while. Try to get some rest."

I shook my head so adamantly that my neck ached in response. "I'm not going to rest until Ruth is found. But if *you* need to—"

"I'm fine." Michael's hand came down on my arm, as if to jolt me back to reality. "I'm just worried about you."

His concern was sweet, but I didn't want to waste any time focusing on me. "How did someone send me that text from Velma?"

"They must have cloned her phone," Michael said. "This person wanted to lure you out so they could threaten you."

"And possibly distract me while they grabbed Ruth." Nausea roiled in my stomach. I still wasn't certain this secret boyfriend was responsible for her disappearance. "What should we do next?"

Michael let out a long breath and glanced ahead, as if gathering his thoughts. "How about if we check on your mom and then go into the office? It's almost morning, and we could use Oscar's help."

My gaze shot to Michael's. I wanted to see the truth there, to know what he really thought. It felt like so much hinged on my next decisions.

"What do you think?" I started. "Should I tell Oscar about my dad? If I tell too many people, then I'm going to have to tell my mom. There's no way around it."

Michael remained stoic for a minute as he seemed to sort his thoughts. "I can't make that call for you, Elliot. But I really think you can trust Oscar." His voice dropped. "On another note, I do think you're eventually going to have to let your mom know, especially if this goes on much longer."

I wanted to argue, but I knew Michael's words were true. I'd known that I couldn't keep this information from my mom forever. I'd just been delaying the inevitable.

"Let me think about it," I finally conceded. "For now,

let's go check on my mom. Then we can go into the office and get busy."

Whoever was behind this was going to pay. I wasn't the violent type, but I'd never before felt a rage like I did now either. That same rage fueled my determination for answers, so I didn't try to subdue it.

No, I needed to use every resource at my disposal.

WHEN I GOT BACK to the house, I was grateful to see Linda doing a wonderful job keeping my mom company. She'd already helped to straighten the house. Most importantly, she'd stayed by my mom's side.

That wasn't to say that my mom was doing well.

No, she probably looked worse than I felt, and that was saying a lot.

But seeing Linda put the gospel into action by showing love to my mom offered me a moment of peace.

That was good. My mom had spent most of her life trying to be the hands and feet of Jesus. It was nice to see someone taking care of her now.

Under the guise of grabbing some Tylenol, I slipped into my room for a minute. Instead of looking for the pain reliever, I leaned against my wall and took a deep breath. How could this be happening? I still couldn't believe it.

I wanted to rewind time. I wanted to go back to when my sister had been at Lily's house. I wanted to change things and make it so that I'd picked her up.

But there was no rewinding life.

A soft knock sounded on my bedroom door.

"Come in!" I called.

Michael slipped inside and closed the door behind him. "Hey, there. Am I interrupting you?"

I shook my head. "No, you're not."

I wished circumstances were different. I wished I could marvel on how handsome Michael was. I wished I could delight in his touch, in the fact that we were dating. I wished I could revel in the giddiness I felt when he was around.

"I'm worried about you." Michael assessed me with his gaze. "This is a lot for anybody, but you've already been through so much."

"Thankfully, I'm not made of glass."

He stepped closer. "But that doesn't mean you're unbreakable. Even the strongest people can only withstand so much pressure."

The next instant, I was in his arms. I let him hold me up—but only for a minute.

I didn't have time to grieve now. This was a time to stay busy.

And I definitely didn't have time to cry, even though tears tried to push themselves out.

He tenderly kissed the top of my head before I stepped back. I appreciated his strength more than I could possibly express to him right now.

"We should get busy." My voice sounded raw as the words left my lips. "Are you ready to head to the office? We can check to see if I missed anything that the Chicken Man left behind."

"Sure. Let's go."

As we stepped toward the front door, my mom called me from the couch where she sat with rumpled tissues surrounding her.

"Find her, Elliot." My mom's voice cracked. "Please."

I stared at her a moment, feeling something unspoken pass between us. Finally, I nodded. "I will."

I dragged my gaze away from her. As I stepped outside, Michael's hand skimmed across my back again.

I was so glad I had him here to hold me up right now. He'd been a real rock in my life ever since I'd met him about two months ago.

Had it really only been two months? Sometimes, it felt like at least a year. Other times, it felt like it had been only days.

Either way, his presence in my life was a blessing.

And, in times like these, a girl had to look for the blessings. Otherwise, she might fall into a pit of despair.

CHAPTER SEVEN

"YOUR DAD WAS A SPY?" Oscar repeated as Michael and I sat across from him in his office.

As the sun had come up, a new workday had started. Even though I felt bleary eyed from searching all night, I knew I wouldn't be resting any time soon.

I stared at Oscar, knowing how outlandish my story sounded. But everything I told him was true.

"That's right." I ignored the sick feeling in my stomach and hoped informing him was the right decision. "I believe part of the reason my family came to this country was because my father needed to escape the new regime that took over in Yerba."

Oscar stared back at me, clearly trying to process my story and form an opinion.

The man was probably forty pounds overweight, with

a round face, a hideous mustache, and a king complex. But he'd apparently been a really good detective at one time. I needed to set my own biases aside if I wanted his help now.

He didn't even reach for his stash of pistachios like he always did while we talked to him. I took that as a sign that he was taking this seriously.

Oscar let out a grunt and leaned back in his chair. I gave him another moment, knowing it was a lot of information to sort through.

"You've known this for a while?" Oscar finally said, his eyes narrowed.

"Yes, but you have to understand that I can't share this information with just anybody." I rubbed my hands across my jeans, trying to keep my nerves under control. "If my father truly was a spy, then my family is a target—especially if Papa left some type of information that the bad guys want."

Oscar tapped his fingers against the desk. "But you're also saying that somebody broke into the office last night dressed like a chicken and threatened you because they want some kind of information that was on a jump drive."

I hated how crazy this all sounded. Those details almost made my story seem less credible. Maybe they'd planned it that way.

And now my sister was missing. I'd sound crazy, if that's what I had to do in order to find Ruth.

"We checked the office when we arrived, but we didn't see any evidence this man left behind," Michael said.

"How about the security cameras?" Oscar asked.

"You're the only one with access to those."

That's right! There were security cameras outside the office.

I watched as Oscar turned to his computer and tapped on the keyboard. A few minutes later, he grunted.

"What is it?" I asked.

"They're black," he muttered.

Michael crossed to the other side of the desk so he could see. Then he grunted also. "Someone must have spray-painted them."

I closed my eyes, hating that the moment of victory had turned so quickly into defeat. "This guy knew the cameras were there. He's always one step ahead."

"I'll check with some other local businesses and see if they have any cameras that picked up anything," Oscar said. "In the meantime, is there any other reason your sister may have been grabbed—if that is, indeed, what happened?"

I sent a nervous glance Michael's way. "Michael and I also discovered that my sister was secretly seeing someone she met online, presumably someone who's older than she is. I suppose it's a possibility that two separate crimes occurred."

I didn't really believe that, but I wanted to put everything on the table. That was another American expression I'd recently learned.

Oscar nodded slowly. "Was everything on her computer backed up on the cloud?"

"Now that you mention it, I think that it was." My pulse spiked. I thought I knew where he was going with this. I hoped I was right.

"Maybe you can somehow get into her account and see exactly what she's been doing online lately," Oscar continued.

"That seems like a great place to start," Michael conceded.

"Why don't you do that?" Oscar said. "While you do, I'll casually put in a call to one of my friends at the State Department. I'll see if he knows anything about what's going on in Yerba or if any of the regime is on any type of US watch list. The country is small enough that something like that probably wouldn't make the news. But it seems like something pertinent to this investigation."

"That would be great." I stood and glanced at Oscar, gratitude filling me. He often wasn't the easiest man to work with, but he seemed to come through when people really needed him. "Thank you so much for your help."

"I know you'd do it for me." His gaze locked onto mine. "So just consider it a favor that you don't need to pay back."

Even more gratitude filled me, but I couldn't take time to dwell on it.

Instead, I headed to the office I shared with Michael.

We needed to see if we could access the cloud drive where my sister backed up her files.

Right now, that was our best hope.

———

THIRTY MINUTES LATER, Michael tip-tapped on his keyboard before sitting up straight.

"I've got it," Michael announced.

I slid my chair across the floor until it stopped next to his. "You got into her cloud account?"

"It took a few tries, but I managed to figure it out." Michael leaned closer to the screen. "Her password for the cloud account is different than her password for the computer. You were right—it was your father's birthday."

"I've always known you're brilliant."

He flashed a quick smile before turning back to the computer. "Do you mind if I look through Ruth's personal things?"

"Not if it means finding her."

Before we dove into her email, Velma stepped inside with a bag in hand. "I brought you guys some bagels from the bakery two doors down. I didn't even get them out of the dumpster."

"You promise?" Michael said.

"Scout's honor." She raised her hand. "Truthfully, I did look. And, I've got to say, Elliot, the bakery's dumpster is filled with fresh fruit scraps. You really should check the place out sometime. I know how much you love tropical fruit."

"It's the South American way." I smiled. "And I will check it out—when this is all over." I studied the woman. Her eyes weren't as bright as they'd once been, and that worried me on so many different levels.

"Make sure you get something to eat," Velma said.

"Thanks, Velma. You're a real lifesaver."

The look she gave me made it clear that we were the ones she considered a lifesaver.

What happened to her had bonded the three of us for life. I had no doubt about that.

I pulled out a bagel, mostly out of courtesy, though. As I took a bite, the bread felt dry in my mouth. Nothing would taste good right now.

"Most of these emails are just between Ruth and her friends. A lot of them are talking about school assignments." Michael continued to click on the various messages.

My gaze scanned all the words there, and I desperately hoped for something that would give me a clue as to where Ruth might be.

But there was nothing.

No mysterious dating websites. No password login notifications. No awkward emails that seemed to disguise something more devilish.

Nothing.

I wasn't ready to give up. We still had other things to look through.

Michael scanned her most recent documents, but they were all school assignments.

Again, nothing.

Then he got to her web history. This was the part that both intrigued me and that caused a sickly dread to rise like bile in me. I didn't like digging into my sister's business like this. But I'd do it if it meant that I might find her.

I just hoped that what I found didn't change my perspective of her.

Michael and I looked at her social media first. Nothing there really surprised me. It all seemed the typical teenage angst type of things.

Before we could look any deeper, my phone rang.

It was my mom.

I wondered if she had an update for us.

Quickly, I put the phone to my ear and answered.

But as soon as I heard my mom's voice, I knew that something was wrong.

I braced myself for the worst.

CHAPTER EIGHT

"I JUST GOT a call from the hospital," my mom started.

The only reason the hospital would call was if they had bad news. "Did they find Ruth? Is she okay?"

Michael and Velma sent me startled looks.

I held back the tears that wanted to stream down my face as I braced myself for whatever Mom was about to say.

"She's not hurt, Elliot," Mom continued. "Not that we know of. Someone from the transplant team called to say Ruth's now the next spot on the list."

My spirits lifted with relief, only to sink with apprehension.

We'd been waiting to hear this news for so long now.

But if Ruth was missing . . . then that lung transplant would go to someone else. I didn't know what that would mean for my sister. Would she lose her place and move down the list? If so, how far?

Either way, it didn't matter.

Cystic fibrosis was serious. Ruth needed that transplant to survive.

"We've got to find her, Elliot." Mom's voice sounded hoarse with emotion.

"I know, Mama. I've been doing everything I can. Believe me. We're working right now on various plans to help find Ruth."

"I know you are . . ." She paused. "They also need proof that we can pay."

My stomach clenched. It was one more worry to add to my growing list. We were still forty thousand short of the amount we needed. Even though I'd helped solve a crime recently and reward money had been promised, it was being held up with logistics right now. It didn't appear that I'd get my portion in time.

"I'll figure something out," I assured her, even though I didn't know how I would do that exactly.

"Go back to work then," Mama continued. "I'll let you know if I hear anything else."

I ended the call and shared with Michael and Velma what I'd just learned.

I saw the truth on their faces—the disappointment they felt. They understood how important this surgery was. Now the opportunity might slip through our fingers.

"Look at this, Elliot." Michael nodded at his computer screen.

I leaned in close. Normally, I'd take a moment to revel in Michael's spicy aftershave. But there was no time for that now.

Instead, my eyes scanned the words on the screen.

It was a message my sister had sent to one of her friends.

I feel like my life is falling apart. Everything I love has been stripped away from me, even my dad. Now I can hardly breathe. Sometimes it doesn't even seem like it's worth it. None of this seems like it's worth it.

A dull thud spread in my chest.

What did that mean? Was my sister feeling so much despair that she was ready to just walk away from it all? Or worse . . . was she ready just to end it all?

A cry lodged in my throat. I couldn't think like that.

And I couldn't stop thinking about it either.

"I FOUND IT," Michael announced fifteen minutes later. He was still on his computer, still combing through Ruth's information.

I stared at his monitor, waiting for it to come into focus. Something had Michael excited, and I couldn't wait to see what.

"This is a dating website." Eagerness lilted his voice. "It looks like your sister logged on here with an alternate name."

"Why would she do something like that?"

"Why do teenagers do most of the things that they do?" Michael murmured. "She has several messages, but Ruth blew off most of the guys who tried to connect with her."

"At least there's that." Maybe some of my faith in my sister could be restored.

"But look at this guy here." He pointed at the screen.

I leaned closer so I could see the profile better. The name this guy went by was MamasBoy.

"Why would he go by a name like that?" I asked.

"He's using it as a hook, trying to make it seem like he's a good boy," Michael said. "According to his bio, he likes long walks on the beach, talking by open fires, and walking his dog, Pixie."

I looked at the man's picture again. Ruth's "love match" appeared to be in his early thirties. He wasn't bad-looking with his light brown hair, average build, and bright smile. He listed his hometown as Fredericksburg, a town less than thirty minutes away.

I didn't want to ask my next question, but I had to. "What do the messages between the two of them say?"

"He started their conversation by telling her she's cute."

I already felt sick to my stomach, and we were just starting to read these messages. I took a long sip of my coffee, trying to prep myself for whatever I might learn next.

My eyes went to my sister's picture. The photo made her look older and more voluptuous than she really was. At least she hadn't used her real name. Instead, she'd gone by Daisy Damsel.

Daisy Damsel? I couldn't even waste my energy thinking about that right now.

"She started corresponding with this guy a few weeks ago," Michael continued. "There must have been something about MamasBoy that caught her eye. She quickly shut down all the other men who approached her."

I scanned the messages, trying to figure out what it was about this man that might have gotten Ruth's attention.

Maybe it was the pictures of dogs he'd posted. My sister *was* an animal lover.

Or maybe it was a picture of the man standing with the jungle behind him. Had that reminded her of home?

My instincts went on alert again.

What if this guy was secretly from Yerba? He didn't appear to be Hispanic but . . .

Michael seemed to read my mind. His jaw tightened as he pointed to the background. "I know what you're thinking, but this image was photoshopped."

I looked closer. He was right. Someone had done a decent photo-editing job, but the shadows didn't line up.

"He didn't say anything in any of his messages about Yerba, did he?" I asked.

Michael continued to stare at the screen. "Ruth asked him if he'd ever been there. He said no, but that he loved to travel."

"Did they ever meet?" I could hardly breathe as I waited for the answer.

"It looks like he gave her a ride a few times. She told him that, even though she was nineteen—"

"She said she was nineteen?" My voice screeched up higher. "She's only seventeen."

Michael nodded. "Yes, and she also said she was afraid of driving. On a few occasions, she didn't want to walk and had no one else to call."

"No one else to call? I would have given her a ride." Had I failed her? Had I been so busy with my investigations that I hadn't seen her needs? Had I driven her to do this?

Guilt pounded at me.

Michael nodded. "I know, Elliot."

"How about yesterday?" Pressure mounted inside me as I waited to see what this turned up.

Why would my sister do this? She was a pretty girl. Certainly there were guys at her school she could have been interested in.

Michael tapped a few more things on the keyboard. "There's nothing on here that indicates they got together yesterday. They could have set up something via messaging on her phone. That's something the police are going to have to look into. I don't have access to that."

"I need to set up a fake profile," I announced.

Michael glanced at me. "What?"

"I need to meet him. If I tell him I'm Daisy Damsel's sister, he'll run far away. But if I'm a teenager who's interested in him, he'll be more likely to meet."

Michael stared at me. "Are you sure you want to do this?"

"Positive."

I watched as Michael set up a profile for Puppy-Love23. It only took ten minutes, and the end result was fantastic. Michael used a picture of me he'd taken the past weekend with the sun setting behind me. I looked younger than my twenty-eight years, and I had a feeling that's what this guy liked.

As soon as I had access to the site, I found Mamas-Boy's profile and sent him a message, letting him know I was interested.

Then I leaned back to wait. I hoped this guy didn't take too long to respond. Because I knew how valuable time was at moments like this.

But waiting was harder for me today than it normally

was. In fact, my skin felt like it crawled ahead of me, like it couldn't stand the suspense either.

I let out a long breath. I couldn't just sit here and do nothing while we waited.

Michael had gotten into Ruth's cloud drive, but we hadn't found anything that might be helpful except for this. Was there anything else we needed to look at?

Not that I could think of right now.

As I glanced at the computer screen again, I saw three dots appear in the message box.

I grabbed Michael's arm. "He's writing back."

I froze with anticipation as I waited to see what MamasBoy wrote.

My eyes widened when I read the words.

You're cute.

"What do you want me to say?" Michael asked.

"Tell him I have a thing for older men."

Michael's eyebrows flickered up. "As you wish."

He typed the words in, and we waited for a response. MamasBoy typed back right away.

Is that right?

I nibbled on my lip. His response was lackluster. Certainly, the man had to be on guard. He didn't want to be set up.

"Tell him I'm nervous because this is my first time doing something like this," I said.

Michael typed in the words.

The man responded, "There's nothing to be worried about."

"Tell him, I probably shouldn't be here. This was a bad idea. I just wanted someone to talk to."

A moment later, he responded. "I'm a great person to talk with. Want to meet?"

My heart pounded in my chest. "Tell him I want to meet at The Board Room in an hour and see what he says."

"Let's see if he takes the bait," Michael muttered.

This was our first lead. It could turn out to be nothing.

But either way, I wanted to talk to this guy in person.

CHAPTER NINE

EVERYTHING HAPPENED FAST.

MamasBoy had agreed to meet with PuppyLove23. I'd called Hunter and told him what I'd done. He hadn't been happy that I'd set something up without consulting him, but I wasn't in the mood to apologize.

Instead, Hunter was going to set up some plain clothes officers at the restaurant. He had someone else who was looking into MamasBoy's real identity and background to find out if this guy had a record or not.

As he did that, Velma was trying to make me look like a teenager. It didn't take much effort.

I'd donned some ripped jeans, a T-shirt, and flip-flops. She pulled my long brown hair into two braids on either side of my head. Then she applied some light pink lip gloss and gave me some pointers on looking younger.

Act clueless. Laugh a lot. Keep your eyes big and innocent.

I looked in the mirror over the sink in the small office bathroom and stared at the end result. All I needed to do was remove the unrelenting determination from my gaze, and I'd look the part.

I really hoped this worked.

And I really hoped that this guy could tell me where my sister was.

Michael appeared in the mirror behind me—I'd left the door open. He put his hands on my shoulders and gave me a slight nod. "Are you ready for this?"

"As ready as I'll ever be, I suppose."

"You're going to do great, Elliot."

"No touching coworkers," Oscar yelled from the hallway as he got up to get another cup of coffee. "Haven't I talked to you about sexual harassment in the workplace?"

Michael dropped his hands and gave me a little smile in the mirror. Then he stepped away, muttering an apology—mostly to put on a show for Oscar.

Our boss didn't know the two of us were dating. If we got any more serious, we'd have to break the news to him. I just prayed that Michael and I could both keep our jobs if we did so.

But right now, my paycheck was the least of my concerns.

I glanced at the time on my phone. I was supposed to

meet this guy in forty-five minutes, but I wanted to get to the restaurant early and make sure that everything was in place first.

My heart thumped into my chest as I tried to get myself in the right mindset.

I could do this. Ruth was depending on me.

"Are you ready to go?" Michael stared at me in the mirror.

I pulled myself together and nodded. "Let's do this."

AS SOON AS I stepped into The Board Room, I spotted Detective Hunter. He sat at a table in the distance reading the newspaper and munching on some cheese and crackers.

He glanced over the top of the paper and gave me a subtle nod.

As I scanned everyone in the restaurant, I thought I recognized a couple of officers from the Storm River PD. They all did a good job blending in, however. The average person wouldn't have a clue.

The past hour had been crazy busy. I'd dropped off Michael at his minivan. Then I'd headed to the police station, where an officer had hooked me up with a wire. Everything I said would be heard by Hunter—and numerous other people.

As I did that, Michael, Velma, and Oscar had gone to the restaurant ahead of me and found a seat. I spotted them across the room. The three of them looked casual, like three coworkers on a business outing.

I felt good knowing that I had a backup team in case things went south.

I took a seat at a table by the window overlooking the river. When the waitress appeared, I ordered an iced tea and asked for a bread basket while I waited.

She gave me a strange look as she took my order. She'd seen me here before, but I had never looked like this. Velma had done a good job making me look like a teen. Because of the nerves that I felt right now, I was most likely going to be acting more immature than usual. I was jumpier than a spittlebug in a field of ornamental grasses.

I glanced at the time again.

MamasBoy should be here any moment now.

He's going to be here soon. I don't want to act like a loon. But this guy was a goon, not someone for whom to swoon. What a way to spend my afternoon.

I glanced at the door and tried to remember the tone of the conversations he and my sister had. They'd been flirty. That meant I would probably need to carry on that persona now. If I wanted to get any information from him, at least.

A moment later, the man walked inside, and I rose

from my seat. He was more handsome than I'd thought he'd be. Tall, broad shoulders, thick light-brown hair. He wore jeans and a blue polo shirt that looked neat and well fitted.

All in all, he looked a little too normal for my comfort.

The man's gaze caught mine, and something shifted there.

I stepped toward him and flashed a smile, trying desperately to reassure him.

"I've been waiting for you." I kept my voice light and innocent.

He stared at me another moment, and I wondered if this would work or if he could see right through me.

CHAPTER TEN

MAMASBOY CONTINUED to stare at me, sweat dotting his forehead.

"I don't meet people like this very often," he finally said, staring at me as if trying to figure out if I was trustworthy or not. "And not usually so quickly."

"Then I'm honored you're doing it for me."

More sweat scattered across his skin as he glanced around again. "Maybe this is a bad idea."

"Why would I be a bad idea?" I stared at him and blinked, trying to look as innocent as possible. "You said you wanted to meet me."

"How do I know you're the real thing?" He studied me again.

"We're just meeting for lunch," I told him. "Why is that a reason to be nervous?"

"How old are you again?"

"Nineteen."

Finally, he nodded, some of his nerves seeming to disappear. "Okay then. You're right. We're just eating together."

I smiled, reminding myself to keep in character. "I already have a table."

A grin crossed his face. It was almost as if all of his discomfort disappeared as he saw a new opportunity before him. I supposed there was no crime in liking younger women—as long as they were older than eighteen.

"That sounds good."

I led him to the table, surprised at how quickly my anxiety was dissipating. Instead, it was replaced by the urge to not only learn more about my sister but to take this guy down.

"You just want bread?" He glanced at the basket. "Why don't you let me order something else for you?"

"Sure. Whatever sounds good to you."

"A girl like you needs to eat. What do you like? Fruit? Hotdogs?" He tilted his head as he studied me. "I'm going to guess you're a veggies and ranch dip kind of girl."

"Get out." I widened my eyes in mock amazement. "How did you know?"

"You don't get a figure like that by eating hotdogs all the time." He raised his eyebrows.

A sick feeling formed in my stomach. Maybe this guy was honestly just clueless . . . but maybe he wasn't.

"So tell me about yourself . . ." He leaned closer, his skin still looking pasty and wet.

"Macy," I said. "My name is Macy."

"Macy? It's great to meet you, Macy. You're really pretty."

Anger burned through me at his words, but I held it back. Everything had to be strategic right now.

"There's not much to say." I played with my straw as I stared across the table at him. "I'm nineteen, and I just graduated from Storm River High. I'm already bored this summer, and it just started. People think there's a lot to do around here, but there's not."

"What do you want to do?"

"See the world."

He shrugged. "Then why don't you?"

"My parents would never let me do that."

"You're nineteen. You're old enough to take control of your own life."

I raised an eyebrow. "You really think so? That's not what my mom and dad say."

"I know so." He nodded assuredly. "Your parents . . . they probably think of you as a little girl still. But you're old enough to know when it's time to spread your wings and fly."

"I'm just not sure I'm ready to do that . . . alone." I

slipped my gaze up to meet his. I felt sick to my stomach as I waited for his response.

A smile tugged at the corner of his lips. "Maybe I could help you."

"Maybe we should get out of here then." That's what Hunter told me to say when I wanted out.

MamasBoy nodded, a little too eagerly. "We should."

Just then, Hunter rose from the table behind him. "Police!"

MamasBoy glanced behind him before taking off in a run.

"I DIDN'T DO ANYTHING." Sweat dripped down MamasBoy's face as Hunter cornered him outside The Board Room. "It's not a crime to meet a pretty girl in a restaurant."

"You like them young, don't you, Marcus Fleming?" Hunter growled.

"I knew I shouldn't have come," MamasBoy muttered, casting another dirty look my way. "But I didn't do anything illegal. The two of us were just eating together."

Hunter released his hold, and Marcus turned toward Michael and me, his lungs heaving in and out with exertion. The man was shaken—as he should be.

"We need to know about your relationship with Ruth

Ransom," Hunter continued. "Also known as Daisy Damsel."

The man's face went still. "I don't know who you're talking about."

"We have evidence showing you do," Hunter said. "So why don't you quit playing games and answer my question?"

Marcus let out a long breath, and his shoulders slumped in defeat. "The two of us don't have a relationship. We just talked online a few times."

"You gave her a ride on more than one occasion, didn't you?" I knew I shouldn't insert myself into this, yet how could I not? I was the one with the most at stake here.

Marcus turned his scowl on me. "Who *are* you? She's the one who should be arrested for claiming to be someone she's not."

I wasn't going to bother arguing with him. I knew he was just trying to deflect his bad behavior onto me. "I'm Daisy Damsel's big sister. And she's missing."

His eyes widened again, and he quickly—adamantly —shook his head. "I didn't have anything to do with that."

"Where were you last night?" Hunter continued to push as the three of us surrounded this man.

"I was at home. By myself. Playing video games."

"So you have no alibi?" Hunter continued.

"That's right. I have no alibi." Marcus's face reddened, and he crossed his arms. "But that doesn't mean I'm guilty."

"We're going to need to take you down to the station to ask you some more questions." Hunter took his arm.

"I didn't do anything. I'm telling the truth." Mamas-Boy's voice rose along with his obvious anxiety.

"You're going to have to prove that." Hunter led him to his police cruiser.

I watched as Hunter handed him off to two officers. After talking with them a few minutes, Hunter wandered back over toward Michael and me.

"My gut feeling is that he doesn't have your sister," he started. "We have patrol officers headed to check his house, and we'll check his cell phone records as well."

I nodded, feeling my lungs deflate. "I came to the same conclusion."

That man may be scum, but he hadn't taken Ruth.

"We're doing everything we can to find her," Hunter assured me.

I knew that, even though I felt numb inside. "Thank you."

"Elliot, I'd like to put out an Amber Alert for your sister. Maybe call the media. Kitty Kight even. The more people who have their eyes open for Ruth, the better."

Kitty Kight was a local newspaper reporter I'd worked with on more than one occasion. I knew I could trust her.

"I want to do whatever is necessary to find Ruth," I said.

Hunter nodded. "I'll get the ball rolling then."

"What kind of ball?" And why was he talking about that now, of all times?

"Hunter means that he'll get things started," Michael explained.

"Of course," I muttered. I should have known it was another crazy American idiom.

As Hunter walked away, Michael turned toward me. The sun hit us, already hot for the early June day. Around us, the scent of the river filled the air—briny, slightly fishy, surprisingly comforting and familiar.

Michael started to say something when our coworkers joined us. They'd been close enough to see all of that go down. I was simply thankful that Hunter and Oscar had worked together. The two of them had some kind of history, and I was nearly certain that neither liked the other. At least they'd put aside their differences to help me.

"What now?" I asked everyone.

"Now we need to get back to the drawing board." Oscar frowned, as if he were disappointed also. "My friend with the State Department called back but didn't have any helpful information. I'm sorry."

"Thanks for trying."

Unfortunately, going back to the office and talking things through held no appeal to me whatsoever.

I had to find my sister before it was too late.

AS I STARED at my computer, I felt my despair growing. I'd been doing some research on Marcus Fleming. Hunter had called to say the man didn't have a criminal record and that his cell phone records indicated he hadn't left his house last night. The messages between him and Ruth appeared to be friendly, but no lines had been crossed.

Apparently, he was innocent—at least, innocent in Ruth's disappearance.

I tried to think of something else I could research online, but my mind went blank. I didn't know where to go from here.

As I saw my reflection on the screen, for a moment, it reminded me of Ruth. My heart lurched into my throat.

Where was my sister right now? Ruth was so young, so innocent. She should be reading books and painting her nails and watching her friends play volleyball.

Or she should be in Yerba. She'd loved hiking, shopping at the local markets, and taking dance classes from some of the natives.

I couldn't bear the thought of my sister suffering.

Every time the images filled my mind, I grew sick to my stomach until I thought that I might throw up.

"Hey," Michael murmured beside me.

I glanced up and saw the worry in his eyes. I heard his silent message—the one he'd sent without saying a word. He hated that I was going through this.

I mouthed, "Thank you," to him before standing.

I couldn't stare at this computer screen any longer.

If I could rule out this guy from the internet as being one of the possible suspects, then that left only my family's connection with Yerba and the unrest there as the culprit.

And there was only one person I could think of to have a talk with about Yerba.

A man named Blaine Kingsley.

"What are you doing, Elliot?" Michael rose beside me, his hands going to his hips and a cautious look entering his eyes.

"There's someone I need to talk to—the only person I can think of who might have answers."

"I'll go with you." He grabbed his keys from his desk.

I wasn't going to argue with him. I could use someone with a cool head to balance out my supercharged emotions right now.

Michael told Oscar and Velma what we were doing. They promised they would keep working from the office to find Ruth. I knew that Oscar was trying to acquire some security videos, and that Velma had made calls to all the local hospitals and bus stations. They were trying to cover every possibility.

Michael waited until we were outside and around the corner before he pulled me into a warm hug.

He didn't say anything. There was nothing to say, and I appreciated the fact that he didn't try to feed me platitudes.

After a few minutes, he kissed my forehead and took my hand. He led me to his minivan, cranked the engine, and pulled from the parking lot.

It was only then that he asked, "Where are we headed?"

"To see Blaine Kingsley," I told him.

"You know where to find him?"

I shrugged. "He's without a job right now, so I'm going to try his house again. It's worked for me in the past."

Michael didn't ask any more questions. "Okay. Let's go."

CHAPTER ELEVEN

"ELLIOT." Blaine Kingsley stared at me from inside the massive doorway of his fancy home. "What brings you by?"

The man was in his late fifties, with a shock of dark hair, tanned skin, and a stocky build. He was the type of man who wore cuff links and shiny shoes, and who loved massages to help relax him. At least, that was the impression I had of him after our last meeting.

"My sister is missing." I got right to the point, knowing there was no time to waste.

"What? I'm sorry to hear that. What does that have to do with me?" His gaze went to Michael before traveling back to me.

"I believe somebody from Yerba is responsible," I told him.

Something shifted in his eyes, and he readjusted his stance. "Why would you think that, Elliot? What would your sister have to do with anything there?"

"Someone from Yerba— I don't know who—thinks I have information that I don't have. I believe this person took Ruth as collateral until I hand over what he wants."

Blaine eyed me. "Are you sure you don't have any of that intelligence?"

Was he fishing for information? I didn't want to believe that, but I needed to keep an open mind.

"All I had was a jump drive that was stolen," I explained. "I wasn't able to get anything from it."

"As I said, I'm sorry to hear all this. But I don't know what you want me to do."

"There's only one person I can think of who might have answers. Who might know who these guys are. You. I need your help."

Blaine stared at me another moment before nodding and opening the door wider. "Come in. Let's talk inside."

Michael and I stepped onto the marble floor just inside his house. Blaine motioned for us to follow him into his office, which was right off the entryway.

Michael and I sat down across from him as Blaine lowered himself into a chair behind his massive mahogany desk.

Blaine laced his hands together as he began to

address us. "I know you feel like I'm the only one with answers. But I'm really not sure what I can do."

I didn't believe that for one minute.

I locked gazes with him, hoping some kind of internal lie detector would engage inside me. I had to figure out what he knew—and what was true.

"There's something I desperately need to know, Mr. Kingsley," I began. "Are there people from Yerba currently here in the United States—people who are up to no good?"

I refused to break eye contact until he gave me that answer.

Because I needed to know the truth.

I needed to know what he knew—even if the truth tore me apart inside.

"ELLIOT . . ." Blaine shook his head. "I'm not sure what you want me to tell you. Are there known Yerbian operatives here in the country? They're not going to announce themselves to me if they are."

"You were an ambassador," Michael said. "Certainly, you would have heard some of the scuttlebutt around town."

"There's always talk," Blaine said. "Talk isn't always true."

I leaned closer. "I don't have any time to waste, Blaine. If you know something, I need to know what that is."

He cringed, almost as if he realized what the stakes were. But I had a feeling that the stakes didn't just apply to Ruth. I had a feeling that the stakes were high for him as well. If the wrong person found out that he was blabbing things that he shouldn't be blabbing . . . no doubt that would spell trouble for him.

"I did hear that the new president, Xavier Flores, sent some people here to cover up some of the messes he's made," Blaine finally said.

"What kind of messes are you talking about?" Michael asked.

Blaine sighed. "Information that could paint Yerba in a bad light. The country is already closed to foreigners. But if the US decides to close their trade with them . . . the results could be devastating. And I'm not talking about just for the common people there. But for the rich as well. They depend on the money from some of the exports to sustain their lifestyles."

"Do you have any idea what kind of messes these people might be cleaning up?" Michael asked.

Blaine shook his head then looked at me. "I wish I did. Your father may have known about some of them. I believe he thought your family was in danger and that's why he came here. And I also think that your theory is correct. That's also probably why he died."

BLAINE DIDN'T SEEM willing to share any other information with us. Or perhaps he didn't know anything else.

All this visit had proven was confirmation that there
were Yerbian operatives living here in the US.

But I already knew that.

What I couldn't figure out was what they wanted or
where they might be.

I paused as I stood in Blaine's office. "I know you
claim you don't know who any of these people are. You
told me before that they blend in. But if you had to guess
where I might look for them, where would that be?"

He looked away, as if my question made him uncomfortable. "I don't know . . ."

"What's your best guess?" Michael pushed.

Again, it almost looked like Blaine had an answer but
didn't want to share it.

That was why I wasn't going anywhere until he did.

"Blaine . . . please." I stepped closer, knowing I had to
get through to him. "My sister's life is on the line. She's
next in line for a double lung transplant. If these people
don't kill her, then not having that surgery will."

He let out a long breath but otherwise remained
silent another moment. "There's a restaurant just outside
of Storm River called Shipwrecks. I heard a rumor that
sometimes they like to meet there. I've never been to this

place before. And Elliot . . . these people are not to be messed with."

"I know that. Thank you."

But as I stepped toward the door to leave, the bell chimed above.

Blaine squeezed past me and pulled the door open.

To my shock, I saw Sergio Sanchez standing on the other side.

Sergio . . . my ex-fiancé. The man who had broken up with me by a text.

What was he doing here in the States?

CHAPTER TWELVE

"ELLIOT?" Sergio blurted.

"Sergio?"

"Sergio?" Michael repeated behind me.

"What a surprise," Blaine said. "I see the two of you know each other."

"What are you doing here?" I hardly heard anybody else around me as I stared at him.

"What are *you* doing here?" Sergio echoed.

There were too many questions being thrown out for my comfort. I needed some answers. My head was beginning to spin.

The man still looked . . . handsome. He was suave, with neat dark hair, a dapper style of dress, and a well-groomed appearance. When he spoke, everyone around listened. When he smiled, everyone stared. And when he set his mind to something, there was no changing it.

I'd been smitten with the man and had even felt honored to be his "chosen one."

But none of that had been real. I just couldn't see it at the time.

"I'm here tending to some business," Sergio finally said.

"I thought the borders were closed." My mind raced as I tried to figure out the logistics of his appearance here. It just didn't make sense.

Sergio shrugged, as if him receiving special favors was a given. "I suppose they make exceptions for people in Yerba who are in positions of power."

"Wait." Michael shifted as he turned to face me. "This is Sergio, the guy who broke your heart?"

Broke my heart was an overstatement. It wasn't exactly true. I *had* been pretty devastated, even though I could now see it was all for the best. Still, I didn't want Sergio to know that.

"Please, come in out of the heat." Blaine ushered the man inside and closed the door. "I wasn't expecting to host a reunion here."

I still stared at Sergio, not exactly out of wonder or delight. Mostly out of curiosity and maybe a touch of bitterness.

"And you just happen to show up in Storm River, of all places?" I continued.

"Yes, Storm River. The business I'm attending to is out of DC, but I heard this was a nice place to stay in the meantime."

"Is that right?" My voice made it clear that I was unconvinced. I'd be a fool to believe in coincidences.

"Absolutely." Sergio's gaze traveled up and down as he looked me over. "You look . . . good, Elliot. Really good."

I touched the tips of my hair, trying to remember if I had changed out of my teenage girl costume or not.

I had. I'd taken the braids out of my hair, at least.

I wasn't going to bother to give Sergio a return compliment.

"I still can't believe you're here," I said instead.

"This is a shock, Elliot, I know." He stepped closer and lowered his voice. "Perhaps we could catch up before I leave to go back?"

I had no desire to catch up with him. But that didn't mean the two of us didn't need to talk.

"Let's do that." I grabbed a business card from my pocket. "Call me."

He stored the card in his pocket before glancing back at me and then at Michael. Finally, his gaze met mine again. "I will. And I look forward to it."

MICHAEL and I didn't say anything to each other for a moment after we got back into his minivan. My thoughts still raced.

As if I didn't have enough problems, Sergio had to show up in the middle of them.

"What are the odds that both of our exes would show up within two weeks of us starting to date each other?" Michael finally said.

I rubbed my temples as a throb began there. "My thoughts exactly. I can't believe Sergio is in Storm River."

"Do you think he's telling the truth?"

"I don't believe anything Sergio says. He always has an agenda."

"Do you think his presence here has anything to do with your sister's disappearance?"

I sucked in a breath at Michael's question. Sergio was many things. He used people to get ahead. He was arrogant. Selfish. Enamored with anything shiny.

But I couldn't see him as a killer.

"I don't think so," I finally said. "But I am interested in seeing who he's going to meet while he's in town."

"Do you think one of those people might lead you to your sister's location?"

"I think it's a good possibility."

As I said the words, Michael pulled out his phone.

"What are you doing?" I asked.

"I'm going to see if Oscar or Velma can sit outside

Blaine's house. When either of them leaves, I want someone to follow him. You and I have too many other things to do."

"That's a good idea."

Once again, I was so thankful to have Michael on my side. I felt like with him as my partner, we could do anything.

Including finding my sister.

CHAPTER THIRTEEN

AS MICHAEL and I headed to Shipwrecks, I couldn't stop thinking about Sergio.

I knew my thoughts should be on my sister. And they were.

But Sergio . . . I never thought I'd see him again. Especially not here. Not now.

He'd broken off our engagement via text. The worst part had been that I had worked for him. When I'd shown up for work the day after our breakup, I'd found out Sergio had transferred me to a different office within the government. He'd effectively figured out how to avoid me after he had broken my heart.

When the two of us had first started dating, our time together had been amazing. He'd been charming, sweet, attentive. Things had moved quickly, and we had gotten engaged four months later.

We'd done that, despite my family's protests. Neither my mom nor dad approved of the two of us dating. Which was why Sergio and I hadn't told them when we had gotten engaged.

Even though Sergio had given me a ring, I wore it on a necklace whenever my parents were nearby. They'd been under some stress, and I'd been waiting for the right time to tell them.

But it never came. That was why, when Sergio called things off, my parents hadn't been able to understand why I hadn't been acting like myself.

I knew I'd created these problems for myself. There were times I wished I could be bolder, that I could simply speak what was on my mind without worrying about the consequences. But then I remembered people's feelings, and I wanted to protect those I cared about from being hurt. I didn't want my decisions to harm others.

And because of that, I'd found myself in a quandary more than once.

"Hey," Michael murmured. "What are you thinking about?"

I pressed my lips together, trying to sort my thoughts before sharing them. Finally, I released a long breath and started. "Michael, I'm not the type of person who thinks that the stars line up against you. But first Roxy shows up and now Sergio? I think we're having the worst luck ever."

"There's no luck involved here."

I studied his face, trying to read what he was thinking. "Then what's going on?"

"Life can throw us whatever obstacles it wants—exes, trouble, danger, sickness. Throughout all those things, there's no doubt in my mind that I want to be with you, Elliot."

Despite everything going on, my heart warmed at his words, at the reminder of just how deeply Michael cared about me. "I want to be with you too."

He squeezed my shoulder before letting his hand trail down my arm. "Then there's nothing to worry about. Sergio's here, but you're going to be okay. *We're* going to be okay."

As much as I wanted to believe his words, there was more at stake here. "We might be okay—we *will* be okay —but I still need to deal with him."

A frown flickered across Michael's lips. "You really want to meet with Sergio?"

I realized I hadn't explained myself earlier. "I don't want to talk to Sergio about our past or anything personal. But I find his appearance here suspicious. Maybe Sergio knows of other people here from Yerba. Maybe there's something he can tell me that will help us find my sister."

Michael's jaw tightened, as if he didn't like that explanation.

"He wouldn't hurt me." But I felt like a hypocrite as I said the words because obviously the man *had* hurt me. But Sergio would never hurt me *physically*.

Michael let out a long breath and turned away, as if gathering his thoughts. "I just don't like any of this, Elliot. What Blaine said was right. These guys are dangerous. They're not going to let anything stop them from getting what they want."

"If I had what they want, I would give it to them."

Michael turned back toward me and studied my face. "Did your dad leave anything else for you, somewhere he could have hidden some type of information?"

"Just that jewelry box with the journal. But I've combed through that journal many, many times. There's nothing there. I even tried to figure out if it might be some kind of cipher. But there was nothing."

"Except a jump drive."

"Except for the jump drive." I frowned. "But these guys have got to know I don't have that anymore. They are the ones who stole it."

Michael shook his head and stared out the window again. "I only wish that Grayson had been able to retrieve something from it before they took it. It would have made our lives a lot easier."

"Isn't that the truth?"

We sat there in silence for a minute, each absorbing everything that had happened.

"We're going to need a lot more than our own strength right now, Michael," I finally said. "We're also going to need a whole lot of prayer."

He squeezed my hand again. "Yes, we are. There's no denying that. We won't get through this while leaning on our own understanding."

At his words, I closed my eyes.

Dear Lord, please help us now. I plead for You to intervene . . . to save my sister . . . to let her get that surgery in time . . . and to make the money we need readily available.

WE PULLED UP TO SHIPWRECKS. The restaurant looked surprisingly innocuous with its blue siding and understated nautical theme. Some fishing nets had been strung across the front of the building and a few buoys hung from the posts near the front door.

The place was located on the water about a mile outside of town and seemed like the type of establishment that blue-collar workers might frequent. It wasn't fancy, and I could already smell the scent of fried seafood drifting from the kitchen.

Pickup trucks filled the lot beside us, and fishing boats came and went from the docks.

Could this place really be where these men plotted their evil deeds?

It was worth a shot.

"I think we should call Hunter." Michael stared at the building in the distance. "If these guys are inside and if they're as dangerous as Blaine said, they're going to be more than you and I can handle."

"I agree." I pulled my cell out but, before I could dial Hunter's number, my phone rang.

It was my mom. I wondered if she had an update.

"Can you call Hunter while I talk to my mom?" I asked.

Michael nodded and pulled out his own phone.

As he did, I put the cell to my ear. "Mama. How are you?"

I was worried about her. Really worried. Part of me wanted to be home with her, but I found comfort in knowing that her friends were there instead.

"Have you found anything yet?" she rushed.

How much did I tell her? I couldn't keep silent about everything. That wouldn't bring her any comfort. But I knew I needed to tread carefully.

"You'll never believe this, Mom," I finally started. "Sergio Sanchez is in town."

"Sergio? There's a name I hoped to never hear again."

Her words only reminded me of just how much she did not like the man.

"Why is he here?" she continued.

"He said he has business to attend to."

My mom practically snorted. "I don't believe a word that man says. You don't think he has anything to do with Ruth's disappearance, do you?"

"We're still trying to figure all that out. We managed to break into Ruth's computer, but we didn't find anything that led us to any answers." I kept quiet about the man my sister had met through the dating site.

My mom would *not* take well to that news. What parent would? Mama was already dealing with so much right now. There would be time to share that update later —once Ruth was safe.

"We have to find her, Elliot." My mom's voice broke.

I held the phone tighter as emotion welled inside me. "I know, Mama. I'm doing everything I can. I promise."

"And be safe, Elliot. I couldn't handle it if something happened to you also. You know that, right?"

Resounding concern stretched her voice, and I knew her words were true. For my mom's sake, I had to watch my steps.

Because the last thing I wanted was to leave my mom all alone in this world.

CHAPTER FOURTEEN

AFTER I ENDED THE CALL, I turned toward Michael.

Before I could say anything, he asked, "How's your mom?"

His thoughtfulness didn't go unnoticed. I appreciated the fact that he seemed to truly care about my family.

"As well as you might imagine." I shifted in the seat, turning away from the sun as it glared into my eyes. "She's struggling."

"As to be expected."

My throat burned. I didn't want to risk losing it right now. There was no time for that.

Instead, I cleared my throat and turned my thoughts back to the case. "What did Hunter say?"

"If we're going inside that restaurant, he wants to go with us. He also told me he'd use discretion and not tell anybody else because he knows how important it is to you to keep this part of your life quiet for now."

Relief hit me. I was so thankful to have an ally in the police department.

But I could also feel the pressure mounting. How much longer could I keep my Yerbian secrets quiet? I didn't know. The truth was bound to escape sooner or later.

"So what are we going to do once we go inside?" I tried to think things through.

"The first thing we do is use our best weapon."

"What's that?" I seriously had no idea what Michael was talking about. I didn't carry a gun or anything.

"You."

I pointed to myself. "Me?"

He wasn't making any sense.

"Yes, you. You need to do what you do best."

"And that is . . .?" I didn't want to sound stupid here, but he'd lost me.

"Observe. Study. Take notes."

I nodded slowly. I couldn't argue with that. I was pretty good at doing those things. I'd just been hoping for something more powerful.

"I can do that," I finally said. "But Blaine said these guys blend in. I might not be able to pick them out of a crowd."

Michael leaned closer, his gaze capturing mine.

"Listen to your instincts. If these guys are from Yerba, maybe you can pick up on something that will identify them."

I rubbed my hands against my jeans, feeling myself starting to sweat. "Or maybe I'll see some recognition in their gaze. They obviously know who I am."

"That's right." Michael nodded, seeming content to know I was catching on. "We'll see what we can find out."

Doubt pummeled me, and I frowned.

What if I failed? What if I couldn't do this?

"Are you sure you're up for this?" Michael stooped, his gaze meeting mine as he seemed to pick up on my self-doubt. "Because Hunter and I can go in by ourselves—"

"No, I want to do this," I told him. "I need to do this not only for Ruth's sake, but for my father's sake. This has all gone on for too long, and I can't sit back any longer, just watching it happen."

Michael leaned toward me and planted a quick kiss on my lips. "You're a strong woman, Elliot Ransom."

I hoped I could live up to his words.

───────

MY HEART SANK in disappointment as we walked into the restaurant.

Only two other patrons were inside—a man and

woman at a corner table who stared at each other as if no one else existed.

I seriously doubted they were the people we were looking for.

Despite that, Hunter, Michael, and I got a table and ordered a quick appetizer—onion rings. My companions insisted that I needed to eat something in order to keep up my energy. But the thought of food in my stomach made me want to puke.

I picked up an onion ring and pulled it apart, watching as the crisp coating separated from the limp onion. I felt a bit like this appetizer—strong on the outside but withered at my center.

I glanced at Hunter, knowing he'd dropped everything to come out here and meet us. He could have been doing other important things to solve this case. "I'm sorry we wasted your time."

Hunter shook his head. "It's not a waste of time, Elliot. I'm glad you called me. I'd much rather be in the loop than have to deal with the aftermath of things when they go south."

His words echoed in my head. He sounded sincere. And, even if we weren't dating, I knew he cared about me as a friend. That went a long way.

"Any leads?" I forced myself to take a sip of water.

"We checked some security footage and talked to all of Ruth's friends. So far, we haven't found anything."

The sick feeling in my stomach intensified. That was what I feared. No answers.

Hunter leaned toward me with his arms on the table. "Elliot, have you told your mom what you know yet? Does she have any clue about your father?"

I shook my head, probably a little too quickly. "I haven't been able to tell her the news."

"You might need to." He gave me a pointed look.

"Why would you say that?" I tried to understand where he was coming from.

Hunter grabbed his own onion ring. "What if she knows something?"

"My mom doesn't know anything," I quickly told him.

"You can't be certain of that. Your mom could be a wealth of information. Maybe she knows of other people from Yerba who are here. I didn't want to bring up Yerba with her when I talked to her last night. But I might need to. I don't know if you're doing yourself any favors by keeping this quiet."

Michael rubbed his hand across my back, as if he sensed my internal distress.

"Elliot will do the right thing," Michael said. "She always does."

"I'm not saying she won't," Hunter said. "I know Elliot well enough to know she's virtuous. But sometimes when you're in the middle of a situation, you don't think clearly."

"This is just a lot to throw on my mom. Maybe I should've told her sooner, before all this trouble started. However, I had no idea that things would turn out this way."

"Think about it," Hunter said. "But don't think too long."

I nodded, the action feeling somber. "I will. I promise."

I had a lot of decisions I needed to make.

But I felt like if I made one wrong decision, everything could come tumbling down.

CHAPTER FIFTEEN

MICHAEL and I headed back to the office to see if Velma had any updates. Oscar was still sitting outside Blaine's house, waiting for either Blaine or Sergio to leave.

Sergio must have made himself right at home. The thought of the two of them being buddy-buddy left me uneasy.

As soon as Michael and I walked into the office, Velma stood from her desk and her gaze latched onto ours. "Anything new?"

"Not really." I paused beside her. "We still haven't found Ruth."

She frowned and rubbed my arm. "I'm so sorry."

I nodded, having no words for the moment.

Velma leaned closer and lowered her voice. "I thought I'd let you know that you have a visitor."

Just as she said the words, the door to the bathroom opened and Grayson Whittier stepped out.

Grayson . . . Michael's contact, a CIA employee, and a computer genius. When he'd tried to break into the jump drive my father had left, he'd been abducted. I was still thankful that he'd managed to get away with his life, however.

He paused near us, tossing the paper towel he dried his hands with into a nearby waste basket. The man was on the shorter side, with thick glasses and blond hair cut short in a no-fuss type of style. Based on his expression, something was wrong.

"Grayson." Michael stepped toward him. "I wasn't expecting to see you here."

"Can we talk?" Grayson didn't bother to smile. Instead, his gaze traveled to me. "All three of us?"

"Of course." I gave Michael a nod.

We went into the enclosed office Michael and I shared, and Michael shut the door behind us. We pulled our chairs together and waited to hear what Grayson had to say.

"I feel like my timing is bad," Grayson started, that grim expression still on his face as he turned to us. "Everyone seems on edge."

"My sister is missing," I told him.

He apparently hadn't heard that news yet. Then again, why would he have? The story hadn't been leaked to the press. Unless he was following our moves, there was no reason for him to know.

I hadn't seen any Amber Alert yet, nor had I been contacted by Kitty Kight.

"I'm really sorry to hear that, Elliot." Grayson's voice took on a somber tone. "I can come later if it's better."

"No," I insisted. "I want to hear what you have to say. If you came all the way here, then it has to be important."

He shifted, pressing his hands across his jeans, almost as if his palms were sweaty. "I keep thinking about when I was abducted. So much of that time is hazy, but occasionally a flashback will hit me. A new memory came to me, and I wanted to share it."

I could hardly breathe as I waited to hear what he had to say. Maybe this was the information we'd been looking for.

"What's going on?" Michael leaned forward.

Grayson rubbed his hands against his jeans again. "I remembered a conversation I heard these men having. They said something about a list they were looking for."

"A list?" My heartbeat pulsed in my ears as I repeated his words.

"That's right. I didn't hear anything else, so I don't know many details." He shrugged, his body still tense. "I'm not sure if that means anything to you. But I just wanted to pass that along, in case it did."

"I have no idea what kind of list that might be. It must

have been on the jump drive." Regret filled me as I thought about the device.

All the answers we needed seemed to be on it.

Of course, we would never know that for sure, not now that the device was gone.

"This must have seemed truly important if you came all the way out here to tell us instead of calling," Michael said.

"After you find cameras in your house and a tracker on your car, you start to get a little paranoid. I don't trust that anything I say on the phone is private." Grayson rubbed the front of his shirt, as if wiping off a bug. "I thought I'd be able to jump right back into life after everything that happened. But it hasn't been that easy."

"It never is." Sadness stretched through my voice. I understood the sentiment all too well. "Thank you for letting me know. If there's anything else you remember, I would love to hear it."

Grayson nodded slowly. "I hope you find your sister."

"Me too."

As we wrapped up the conversation, my phone rang.

It was Sergio.

This day kept getting worse and worse.

"ELLIOT . . . I was hoping we might meet for dinner," Sergio started.

I glanced up at Michael, watching as he started to walk with Grayson toward the front door.

"Dinner?" I made sure to say loud enough for Michael to hear. "When are you thinking?"

"Tonight. Is that okay?"

I pressed my lips together. I had no desire to spend time with this man. But if there was any possible chance he had information I could use, I couldn't turn it down.

The timing seemed awful—unless his appearance here was connected with Ruth's disappearance. If that was the case, I needed to find out what he knew.

To my knowledge, Sergio didn't know that Ruth was missing—unless Blaine had told him.

"That sounds good," I finally said. "Where are you thinking?"

"I am not really familiar with this area," Sergio said. "Do you have any recommendations? The meal is on me."

"Sure. Let's meet at The Quarterdeck."

I almost said The Board Room, but I didn't want to fill my favorite restaurant with bad memories. Instead, I picked a place where Oscar had taken the staff once. The Quarterdeck was more upscale, but, since Sergio was paying, I didn't care.

"Great," he said. "Can we meet at six?"

I glanced at the time. That would still leave me an

hour before I had to be there. "Six sounds good. I'll see you then."

As I lowered my phone, I saw Michael had walked back into the office and was staring at me. No doubt he was wondering what that conversation was about.

He wasn't the insecure type, so I doubted he felt threatened right now. But did any guy want to see his girl-friend going to dinner with an ex? Probably not.

"Sergio?" Michael watched me carefully for my response.

"I'm going to meet him for dinner. I want to see if he knows anything."

"Do you want me to go with you?"

I thought about it for a moment. I could really see the outcome going both ways. Sergio might be more inclined to speak with me if I was alone. But I didn't want him to think that I was interested in him either.

I let out a long breath. "I don't want to go alone, but I have a feeling he'll be more open if I am."

Michael frowned. "I don't really want you to go alone either, especially since we don't know who is behind all of this."

Hearing the theory voiced aloud drove home reality and made me suck in a breath. "You think Sergio might be behind Ruth's abduction?"

Michael locked his gaze with mine. "He's here at just the wrong time, isn't he?"

"Yes, he is."

"How about this?" Michael finally said. "I'll be at the restaurant. I'll change up so Sergio won't recognize me. But I would like to be close, just in case."

Just in case . . . just in case what? Things turned ugly? Someone tried to abduct me also? Sergio busted a move?

Maybe all those things.

"That sounds like a great plan," I said. "Thank you, Michael."

"I'll do everything within my power to help you find your sister."

CHAPTER SIXTEEN

THIRTY MINUTES LATER, I changed into a red dress I kept in the closet at the office. When I first started working here, Michael and Velma had suggested I keep a few changes of clothes on hand, just in case I needed them. It looked like they were right.

I'd worn this dress to a fundraiser when I first started working for Driscoll and Associates. The front came down in a V-neck, and the bodice hugged me "in all the right places," as Velma said. But the outfit still retained a level of modesty. Nothing about it was too short or too plunging.

When I stepped out from the bathroom, Michael let out a low whistle. "Elliot . . . you look . . . great."

I was pretty sure I blushed.

He took my hand and gave me a twirl on the floor.

Thankfully, Oscar wasn't here to see any of that or he would be spouting off something about sexual harassment again.

But as I glanced over at Velma, she smiled and quickly looked away.

I had no doubt she suspected something was going on between the two of us. We would need to be more careful.

Michael didn't look like himself either. Normally, he liked to wear T-shirts and jeans with his baseball hat. But he'd changed into black dress slacks, a button-up white shirt, and shiny dress shoes. I wasn't the only one who was capable of transforming into someone different.

"We should probably drive separately, just in case Sergio sees us pull up," Michael said.

"I agree," I said.

"I called Oscar. He said Sergio left five minutes ago."

I ran my hand across the front of my dress, pushing down the quell of nerves I felt. "Then we should probably go."

"You two be careful and have fun," Velma called.

I wasn't sure that fun was the word for the situation.

But I did hope that this meeting was fruitful.

My sister's image appeared in my mind again. I prayed Ruth was okay. I also prayed that all this wasn't for nothing.

I RAN my hand across my dress again as I stepped into the restaurant. I hadn't expected to feel this nervous. But there was so much at stake here.

If I were honest with myself, I'd admit that it was more than being nervous because of Ruth. Meeting with the man who'd broken your heart was neither easy nor fun. But I'd do whatever was necessary to help Ruth right now.

Michael was going to come in a few minutes behind me. Hopefully, Sergio would be so distracted by talking to me that he wouldn't even notice—or recognize—Michael.

We hoped our plan worked, at least.

Please, don't let me fail. The bad guy needs to go to jail. Were we even on the right trail? Would the truth prevail?

The Quarterdeck was one of the fancier seafood restaurants in the area. A harpist played in the corner, the lights were dim, and windows stretched across an entire wall.

The place even smelled expensive, with tinges of rich butter, fresh herbs, and baked bread.

I approached the hostess and told her who I was meeting. She smiled pleasantly as she led me to a table near the window. Her gaze lingered on Sergio just a moment too long.

She found him attractive. Most women would. I'd certainly fallen under his spell.

When Sergio saw me, a smile filled his face. "Señorita, you look . . . *hermosa.*"

My cheeks heated. "Thank you."

"Have a seat." Sergio helped me to my seat before taking his place across the table.

I nervously tucked myself into the chair, memories of our time together in Yerba battering me. Dinners like this weren't unusual back then. Usually, Sergio had combined them with business. I'd been by his side, a dutiful employee who helped him remember names and birthdays.

I'd made him look good. No one could deny that.

Then, when we'd been alone, he'd wooed me and swept me off my feet.

But it had all been a lie.

Sergio picked up his menu. "Everything smells delicious. I'm going to have to rely on you to tell me what I should order. What's good here?"

"You can't go wrong with the crab cakes," I told him.

He cast a sharp glance my way. "Did you forget that I have a shellfish allergy?"

I hadn't. Shame on me. But I wouldn't have actually let him eat them.

Most likely.

"Then I would try the mahi," I said instead, the soothing sounds of the harp softening my words. "I've heard it's delicious."

"That is what I will get then." Sergio closed his menu.

The server came and took our orders.

When she left, Sergio focused his gaze on me. "You look like you've really adjusted well to life here in the States."

"I don't know if I'd say that, but there's no need to look back when I'm only moving forward." My words were purposefully pointed.

Sergio nodded his head with a little twist. "Of course. I was so sorry to hear about your father."

My throat burned when I heard him talk about my dad. So Sergio *had* known what happened to him. He had never bothered to call or send a card. This once again showed his character and made me dislike him even more.

I glanced over as someone was seated behind Sergio.

Michael.

He sat with his back toward us, just in case Sergio turned around. I already felt better, knowing he was there.

"My father's death was a big loss to all of us." My neck stiffened as I said the words. "I still can't believe he's gone."

"He was a good man. I am honored to have met him, even if he never did like me."

I wanted to say something smart back, but I didn't. Instead, I rested my hand on the silky linen tablecloth.

Sergio was made to go to places like this. I wasn't.

"Any updates on your sister?" Sergio took a sip of his drink. "Blaine told me about Ruth. I'm very sorry to hear this. I know the two of you are close, and I know my timing today must seem awful."

"No, we haven't heard anything. And I figured meeting with you would be a nice break from worrying."

He studied me, as if trying to ascertain the truth in my words. "You must be beside yourself."

"To say the least," I said. "I just keep praying that the police find her."

"Who would've done such a thing?"

"That's what we're all wondering." But as I said the words, familiar thoughts slammed into my mind again.

What if Sergio had something to do with it?

Somehow, I needed to figure out the answer to that question.

CHAPTER SEVENTEEN

"WHAT ARE you doing now that you are here in Storm River?" Sergio placed his napkin in his lap as an appetizer was delivered. Bruschetta. It was one of the only things we could order without shellfish. We couldn't have crab dip, shrimp cocktail, oysters Rockefeller, or clam chowder.

I wasn't sure how much I really wanted to tell Sergio about my life. For me, this wasn't a social call. I didn't want to catch up and pretend we were still friends. But I had to play nice if I wanted some answers.

"I'm an assistant to a private investigator, actually," I told him.

He raised his eyebrows. "How interesting. But I can see that you would be good at that job. You have always had a good attention to detail."

Sergio was a charmer, that was for sure. And here he was now, trying to make me believe that he thought highly of me.

You didn't break up via text with someone you thought highly of.

"What about you? Are you still working for the new government?" Bitterness filled my mouth as I casually asked the question.

One side of Sergio's face twisted, as it always did when he was uncomfortable. I used to remind him that action was his tell whenever he was tempted to lie, and, if he wanted to continue in politics, he needed to watch it.

I wasn't surprised to see he hadn't taken my advice.

"I am," Sergio said. "Things have been rough, but we are holding on. Good changes are coming."

"Have people begun to realize that their rights have been taken away from them for what leaders are calling 'their own good'?" I had to ask the question. I didn't like what my home country had become, and I couldn't pretend I did.

His gaze darkened, but only for a moment, before his charm returned.

"Of course, that is not the way we see it. We are trying to help all the people." Sergio wiped his mouth with his napkin. "But I did not want to meet with you so we could argue. I wanted to see how you are doing."

I highly doubted that. I took a long sip of my water,

suddenly feeling thirsty—and anxious to get this over with.

"I've been better, to say the least," I said. "A lot has happened."

"Indeed."

I leaned closer. "Say, is there anybody else you know here in the States? Anyone from Yerba? I know you have a lot of contacts through your job."

His eyes narrowed in thought. "There are a few people. Like Blaine, for example. Why would you ask?"

I studied Sergio's face, wondering exactly how much he knew. The man looked composed enough—not like a guilty man.

But that didn't mean he wasn't.

I had to make a quick decision as to whether or not to make up a story or to just dive in with the truth. I didn't want to show my hand, but I also didn't want to miss an opportunity.

"I suspect that my dad had enemies back in Yerba," I finally said. "I suspect his enemies might have followed my family here." I decided to go with the truth. I just had to be careful not to divulge too many details.

"Your dad had enemies?" Sergio studied me, his expression otherwise unreadable.

I nodded, studying his face also.

I felt like we were having some kind of standoff,

waiting to see who would draw their weapon first—their weapon being the truth.

"You already knew that, didn't you?" I finally said.

Sergio didn't deny it. Instead, he took another bite of his bruschetta as if this dinner were casual.

"You do not work for a government without making some enemies, I suppose," Sergio said.

Did Sergio know what my dad's real job had been? That was the question. I felt confident he did. But I wasn't sure I could risk asking, just in case he didn't.

"Who else do you know here?" I got right to the point. My sister was missing. There was no time to waste here.

"Nobody who would have killed your father, if that is what you are asking." Sergio let out a brittle laugh.

I didn't laugh with him. "I want their names."

His grin disappeared. "You are serious?"

"Dead."

He put down his bruschetta. "I do not like the sound of this, Elliot."

"I don't like the fact that I'm having to live this."

Sergio stared at me another moment before seeming to realize the seriousness of the situation. Finally, he nodded slowly, almost as if resigned. "You are looking in the wrong direction if you think someone I know took Ruth."

Our food was delivered, but my appetite had deserted me. Just to be polite, I picked at the grilled halibut I'd ordered. But part of me was ready to get out of here. Not only was I exhausted, but my lack of sleep was catching up with me. My thoughts were starting to collide inside me and not make sense.

Sergio leaned closer and lowered his voice. "Elliot, I have been meaning to tell you . . ."

I wasn't going to let him off the hook. He needed to finish that statement, no matter how awkward he might feel. "Tell me what?"

"I am sorry that things went the way they did."

My heart hardened in my chest. "Do you mean you're sorry you broke up with me via text message? And then transferred me out of the office? And then never spoke to me again?"

Sergio had the sense to look a little awkward and slightly ashamed at my words. "It was not my best moment."

"I'd say." I gave him a hard stare.

"But there was a lot going on with the government at the time," he explained. "I just could not add another complication."

"That's good to know that I was a complication in your life."

"Elliot . . ." Sergio reached across the table for my hand, but I pulled it back. His eyes widened at the rejection, but he slowly nodded. "I deserved that."

"You deserve a lot more than that." I put my fork

down, unable to continue with this fakery. "You know, it was good to catch up with you for a few minutes. But I need to get going."

"Are you sure?" He truly sounded shocked, like he couldn't imagine why I wouldn't want to be around him.

"I need to find my sister. And check on my mom. Would you mind writing down those names for me before I leave?"

He studied me another moment before nodding. Then he pulled some paper from his jacket, as well as a pen. He wrote something and handed the sheet to me.

"Good luck," he muttered.

I gripped the piece of paper in my hand as if it was a lifeline. I started to tell him that it was good to see him. But the words wouldn't leave my lips.

Instead, I said, "I hope you enjoy your stay in the good old US of A."

And with that, I walked away.

Leaving him in the dust felt good. Really good.

MICHAEL and I had agreed to meet at my mom's place. It would be easier that way, especially since we'd driven separately.

But as soon as we stepped inside my house, my mom

rushed toward me, almost as if she expected me to actually be Ruth coming home.

Her face fell—but only for a moment. The next instant, she pulled me into her arms in a tight hug. She didn't even try to hold back her sobs this time.

"Oh, Elliot."

My throat tightened until I could hardly swallow. I held back my own tears, which only made my throat burn. Between the two, I could hardly breathe.

"No updates?" I asked.

"No. Nothing." She slipped away from me and shook her head before running a finger under her eyes. Then she blinked, her eyes focusing on my outfit. "Why are you dressed like that?"

"It's a long story."

She looked beyond me at Michael. She started to give him a nod, but then pulled him into a hug as well. He didn't let go until she did.

In the middle of all this turmoil, at least there was this. The moment touched me. Mama was showing she'd accepted Michael into our lives, and that meant a lot.

"Thank you for being there for my daughter," she murmured.

"There's nowhere else I'd rather be," Michael said.

I glanced behind my mom and saw a new friend had come to keep her company. I thought her name was Sylvia, but I couldn't remember for sure. I was simply grateful that there had been a steady stream of people here so she wouldn't be alone.

Knowing my mom, she was also stressed about not being able to work. It wasn't that she was a workaholic. We just needed all the money we could get right now in order to pay for my sister's surgery and the follow-up medications.

My sister's surgery . . . was that even going to happen now? And what about the money to pay for it?

I couldn't think about it now.

I paced over to my mom's friend and stood close to her. "Why don't you go home now? I am going to be here for most of the evening. If we need anything, we can call."

The woman nodded, but her own eyes were red as if she had been crying along with my mom. Those were the best kinds of friends, weren't they? The ones who would laugh and cry with you.

She stood and whispered a few things to my mom before they hugged. Then she grabbed her purse and was out the door, leaving just the three of us together.

My mom practically collapsed onto the couch. "I can't stop thinking about Ruth. What if she's suffering right now?"

I sat beside my mom and put my arm around her. "We can't think like that."

"I can't stop thinking like that. I feel like my prayers are falling on deaf ears."

"God has never turned away from you before," I told her. "He is not going to turn away from you now."

She pulled me into another hug. I could feel the sobs from deep inside her.

Another pang of worry rushed through me. It wasn't uncommon in situations like this for loved ones to have some type of medical issue themselves. The stress my mom was under at this point put her at risk.

I desperately wanted to alleviate some of that for her, but I couldn't. I didn't know what else I could do. I'd been out on the streets all day and most of the night trying to find answers. I'd talked to a dating-site loser. A diplomat. My ex-fiancé. A CIA employee.

Yet none of that felt like enough because none of that had produced answers.

"Mama, I really think you should take a shower and try to get a little sleep. I am going to monitor the phones in case there are any updates. I promise I will get you if there are."

"But . . ."

"Please, Mom. You're not looking well. You need to try to rest for a little while."

"I don't want to leave you here alone either."

"I'll stay with her." Michael rested his hand on my back. "If it's okay with you, I would like to sleep on your couch tonight, just so I can be around in case you need me."

I stared at my mom's face, waiting for her to reject that idea. To my surprise, she nodded. "Okay. I'm sure that would be nice. I know that Elliot would like that support."

Mom stood and glanced around once more. Her eyes looked hollow and her motions jerky.

Seeing her like this just made me feel sick inside. And I thought I couldn't feel any sicker than I already did. But I was wrong.

Seeing someone you loved suffer was one of the worst things you could experience, especially when you knew there was no way you could fix it.

It brought me back to the days after my father died. Hadn't my family been through enough? But I reminded myself of what I had just told my mom.

God had never turned His back on us yet.

And He wasn't going to now.

CHAPTER EIGHTEEN

ONCE MY MOM was in her room resting, I collapsed on the couch. Michael pulled me into another hug. He seemed to sense I needed a lot of those today.

And I did.

I was having trouble holding myself together.

"What can I do for you?" Michael murmured into my hair.

That was a great question. I rubbed my temples as I tried to sort out my thoughts. "I guess I just need to talk things through with you. Maybe if I get my thoughts out of my mind, they'll make more sense."

Michael shifted until we could see each other face-to-face. "Then let's talk them through. Do you want to start with Sergio? I loved the way you handled him back there, by the way. You didn't let him win."

"I've wasted entirely too much energy on the man. And if he thinks he can just waltz back in my life and act like nothing happened, he's wrong. Fool me once, shame on you. Fool me twice . . ."

"What about those names he gave you?" Michael asked.

I reached into my purse and pulled out the paper. Michael peered over my shoulder as I looked at the hand-written list. The feel of his body heat next to me brought a surprising comfort. Human touch should never be underestimated.

"Any of them familiar?" Michael asked.

I shook my head. "No, I've already taken a look at them."

"We should probably let Hunter know who these people are."

"I'll give him a call."

Michael rubbed my shoulders, his touch warming me. "At least we have some direction for tomorrow."

"Some direction is better than no direction."

Michael released my shoulders and ran a hand over his face, the action showing just how exhausted he was. "Maybe we should start at the beginning and spell out everything we know. Maybe there's something in the timeline we're missing. In my experience, those details could lead us to the answers we need."

I figured it couldn't hurt and at least we'd be doing

something. "Okay, this is what we know. A new regime took over in Yerba. My family got out just in time. A few months later, after my father died, I learned that he had been a spy for the country. I don't know what kind of information he learned as a spy. But maybe he had some type of state secrets that have made someone feel threatened."

"Okay. Keep going." Michael rolled his finger in the air, as if this could be helping him.

"I now believe that someone knew my father moved here, and they killed him and made it look like a heart attack. I'm not sure exactly why they killed him. Maybe he knew too much information. And maybe it was only after he died that they learned this information had also been stored somewhere else."

"And that's what these men are trying to figure out," Michael finished.

"Exactly. My father must have had contacts in this area because he sent that man to watch me. Unfortunately, the bad guys must have known this, and they killed my father's colleague."

It was another detail in a long list. As a quick recap: One of my father's friends had been found dead behind the stage at a lip-synching competition. We discovered he'd been trying to protect me, but a Yerbian operative had gotten to him first.

"Yes, that's unfortunately true. Don't forget the fact

that during this whole time you felt like you were being watched. And you may, for that matter, have two different groups keeping an eye on you—the people that your father tasked with protecting you and the people who hated your father."

"That's right. So then this man breaks into my office wanting to get information from me—information that most likely is located on the jump drive that was left in my father's possessions at the resort where he worked. This is where it really starts to confuse me. Because if they know I don't have the jump drive and I couldn't access its contents, why would they think I have the information?" I pulled my leg beneath me.

"Because maybe the information was never on the jump drive," Michael suggested, a spark igniting in his gaze.

I let his words wash over me. He might be onto something. "But if it's not on the jump drive . . . where would it be? My family hardly brought anything with us from Yerba. Most of the furniture we own is secondhand. The only things I packed were clothes, a few books, and some pictures."

Michael narrowed his gaze as he stared off in thought. "You said there's nothing in the journal that your father left you?"

I half nodded, half shrugged. "That's right. You're welcome to look at it yourself, but there's nothing on those pages that indicates any type of state secrets. I've been through it multiple times."

"But could there be something on those pages that might indicate where the information was held?"

"I suppose that's a possibility." Anything was a possibility at this point.

Michael turned toward me, a new gleam in his eyes. "Do you mind if I take a look at it?"

"Not at all," I told him. "If you think it could help."

Yet I couldn't seem to move from the couch to retrieve it. I leaned back. My whole body wanted to shut down, along with my mind.

I tried to force myself to stay alert, to stay active.

But my body was winning.

"One more question." Michael narrowed his gaze. "I've been meaning to ask you this, Elliot. Why is your last name different than your father's?"

That was an excellent question, and I was surprised this was the first time it had come up. I pulled my other leg beneath me, ignoring my heavy eyelids. "When my sister and I were born, my mom and dad decided that we should have dual citizenship. And just for the sake of ease, they decided that my sister and I should keep my mom's maiden name."

"Interesting."

"At the time, I thought it was just to make things simpler in case we ever wanted to move to the States. But now I'm starting to wonder if it was to help conceal our identities if we ever moved away. It doesn't appear that it did." I frowned. My dad was a brilliant man. Yet, despite all his planning, we were still in this mess right now.

Some things in life were totally out of our control. Actually, most things were.

"Things will start to make sense," Michael murmured. "They will."

I offered what I hoped was a grateful smile.

"Where's that journal? Why don't you let me get it and you stay here and rest?"

I nodded and told Michael where it was.

But before he could even get back, I rested my head on the pillow.

And everything else faded from my thoughts.

WHEN I AWOKE, Michael sat in the chair across from me and my mom seemed to be aimlessly keeping herself busy in the kitchen.

I pulled myself upright on the couch, feeling like I'd been hit by a ton of bricks. My head pounded, my throat felt dry, and confusion gripped me.

Then everything rushed back.

My sister was missing. We were running out of time to

find her. How could I have fallen asleep in the middle of a crisis like this?

I raked my hand through my hair, wishing this was all a nightmare. But I knew better. I wouldn't be that fortunate.

"Morning," Michael muttered, his eyes still sleepy and his motions slow.

"I slept out here?" I tried to recall what had happened, but everything was hazy.

"I went to go get the journal from your room last night and when I came back you were asleep." Michael shrugged. "I decided just to put a blanket over you and let you stay out here. It rained last night, and I'm pretty sure the sound lulled you to sleep."

I glanced at the window and saw some stray drops drizzling down the glass. "If I slept on the couch, where did you sleep?"

"In the chair." He patted the cushion beneath him.

I could tell by the way Michael said the words—along with his pallid skin—that he didn't get that much sleep at all. I knew what he was sacrificing to help me, and I appreciated it—on top of feeling a touch of guilt.

"Breakfast is ready," Mama called.

I should have known she was cooking. I could smell the aroma of fried sausage in the air. I could hear glasses clinking and pans scraping and eggs sizzling.

I glanced back at my mom as she worked in the kitchen.

I was certain that cooking was a way to distract her from reality. We all needed some type of outlet for these things, and working in the kitchen was one of my mom's.

I wanted to find out how my mom was doing, but I also wanted to talk to Michael. I knew he'd looked through my father's journal last night, and I wondered if he'd seen anything that I hadn't.

For now, I would eat.

I pulled myself to my feet and ambled toward the kitchen table. I saw that my mom had made *desayuno peruano*, a traditional Yerbian breakfast with French bread, pork chicharron, blood sausage, scrambled eggs, and fruit.

Normally, I'd love this. I'd relish the scent of the sausage. I'd crave the freshness of the papaya. I'd savor the taste of the pork chicharron for days.

But not now.

After we sat around the table, Michael said a prayer for us, certain to mention Ruth.

Just hearing her name spoken out loud made everything hit me again. How could this be happening? I really hoped we found some type of direction today, some kind of clue that would lead us to our next steps.

"How are you doing today, Mama?" I stared at her from across the table.

Her eyes looked a little brighter, and her emotions not quite as frantic.

"I spent most of the night on my knees in prayer," she said. "I know that God has got the situation in his hands. But I'm still worried."

"I don't suppose you've heard anything?" I took a sip of the rich South American coffee my mom had prepared.

"I haven't. I was hoping that maybe you would talk to Hunter. But it looked like you needed sleep even more than I did."

I guess I *was* more exhausted than I thought I was. I took another sip of my drink, needing a jolt of caffeine.

Michael remained quiet, letting my mom and me talk. It was weird not having Ruth beside me. She was normally here when we had breakfast together. She was the chatterbox of our threesome, talking about school and friends and extracurricular activities.

As I stared at her empty chair, I fought back tears.

"Bonnie is going to come over this morning." My mom picked at her piece of bread. "I figured that you and Michael would be hitting the streets again."

I glanced at Michael, and he nodded in agreement. "That's the plan. I'm not going to stop until we have answers."

"You mean, until we have your sister back," my mom corrected me with a hard stare.

"Of course, that's what I meant." And I prayed that would be the case.

I had to keep hope alive. My sister would be found alive. Breathing.

There was no other option.

CHAPTER NINETEEN

MICHAEL TURNED to me as soon as we climbed into his minivan after breakfast.

I'd taken just enough time to shower and throw some clean clothes on. I felt a little better—if I could just get rid of the pounding in my head. The Tylenol I'd taken hadn't kicked in yet.

As we sat there, droplets of water still pooled on the windshield, evidence of last night's rain. The whole neighborhood somehow smelled fresher, cleaner, like the ground had needed a good soaking.

Maybe the landscape had needed rain like I'd needed rest, whether I wanted to admit it or not.

As I saw one of Chloe's dolls poking out from beneath the seat, my heart lurched. Chloe . . .

"Have you talked to your family?" I rushed.

Michael blinked. "What?"

"Have you talked to Chloe? Is she okay?"

His hand gently clamped my arm. "I talked to her this morning. She's fine."

I released the tension in my muscles with one big puff of air.

"She's okay, Elliot," he reassured me. "These guys aren't going after her."

"But what if they do?" My voice cracked.

"Oh, Elliot . . ." He pulled me into his arms.

But his reassurances didn't matter to me. I was putting him in a situation that could have serious consequences for his family.

"I won't be able to forgive myself if anything happens to Chloe."

"She's safe . . ."

She was, but for how long? Maybe Sergio had messed with my mind. He'd reminded me about the bad choices that I'd made. I couldn't let Michael or Chloe suffer the effects of one of my poor decisions.

I straightened. I'd have to think about this later. Right now, I needed to concentrate on finding my sister. I wiped beneath my eyes.

"I'm sorry," I started. "Let's talk about today."

Michael stared at me a moment before nodding. "So I researched the men on that list that Sergio gave you."

"And?" I stared at him, anxious to hear if he'd discovered anything.

Excitement lit in his gaze. "Here's the thing. All these men are connected with one person. Peter Harrington."

My eyes widened at the familiar name. Mr. Harrington was one of the wealthiest men in the area. He was single, charitable, and involved in the community. Michael and I had worked with him at a charity softball game not too long ago.

He also owned the resort where my father had worked—the place my father had died as well—along with several other businesses.

"How is he connected?" I asked.

"One of the men works for him. Another went out with Mr. Harrington's daughter. Another has been a guest at his resort."

"So you think Mr. Harrington might be involved?" My throat clogged as I said the words and waited for his response.

"I'm not sure, but it seems like a possibility worth exploring."

I couldn't disagree. "So what next?"

"I say we see what Mr. Harrington is up to. I know where he lives. Let's tail him and see where he goes today."

"Great idea." I nodded. "By the way, did you ever hear

from Oscar? Did Blaine end up going anywhere yesterday?"

"Blaine stayed home all day. I know Oscar was called away to do something at some point, and Velma took his place. But there were no updates."

I appreciated their help. I couldn't have gotten this far without them. "Okay. At least we can pursue Mr. Harrington. Maybe that lead will turn up something."

Michael glanced at me. "Let's hope."

WE SWUNG by Michael's house so he could also get cleaned up. Then we grabbed some coffee from a nearby shop. Michael tried to talk me into a biscuit, but I'd refused. He must have noticed how I'd hardly touched my breakfast back at the house.

We pulled onto the street in front of Mr. Harrington's mansion. Michael had checked with a few of his sources, and it appeared that Mr. Harrington was in town. Since the man ran multiple businesses, he had several homes and often traveled. But it looked like we were in luck today.

As Michael and I sat in his minivan in front of Mr. Harrington's house for a few minutes, waiting to see if anything would happen, another question formed on my lips.

"Did you have a chance to look at the journal last night?" I asked quietly.

"I did. I'm glad you asked. I really wanted to say something earlier, but I knew I couldn't when your mom was there. It's probably nothing, but I did write down a few notes."

"You're keeping me in suspense. What did you discover?"

Michael pulled a piece of paper from his pocket and stared at the words he'd written. "As you know, your dad gave you several pieces of advice. A few in particular seemed key. One was he said to look beyond the obvious. Another: don't be afraid of adversity."

"That sounds like my dad."

"It also sounds like perfect advice for this situation. Another thing he said was that evil men must be put in their places, and things done in the darkness must come into the light."

It did sound like my father was speaking directly toward this situation, as if he feared it might happen.

Michael let out a slow breath and turned toward me. "Here's the other thought I had. Your dad was a smart man. I can tell by what he wrote in the journal. Not only did he love you, but he was one of the best at what he did. Am I correct?"

Warmth filled me when I heard the positive words

Michael spoke about my father. "Yes, I would definitely say that's true."

"Then the only thing I can conclude is that your father was entirely too smart to put any of that information on a jump drive."

I let Michael's words wash over me for a second.

He was right. Absolutely correct.

Why hadn't I seen this sooner?

"Think about it," Michael continued. "Your father left this jump drive in his locker at work. The only reason it wasn't discovered earlier was because the manager put his things in a safe. But as soon as these guys figured out that you might have it, they didn't give up until that device was in their possession. Then your dad made it difficult to figure out whatever was on it. If he really wanted you to get in, wouldn't he have made it more obvious?"

I let his words sink in. They made a lot of sense.

Why hadn't we seen this earlier?

"I think you're absolutely correct," I said. "But if he didn't put this information—this list, let's say—on that jump drive, then where is it?"

"To find that answer, we need to think like a spy."

I let out a long breath, my thoughts racing with possibilities. "Well, in the movies—not that I watch very many —it's always in a secret security box or something. But how do you even find out if somebody has one of those?"

"That's a good question. If he did have one of those, then your dad would have left you a clue as to where it was—I can only assume, at least."

"Or maybe he left this information in plain sight." My mind raced with ideas. "I mean, isn't that something that people do also? They pick the most obvious place because it's the last place that people are going to look."

"That's also a possibility. So my theory is that these guys who were after you finally managed to crack that jump drive. And, when they did, there was nothing there. And that's why they're coming after you now after leaving you alone for a couple of weeks."

The truth spread through me like a nuclear bomb leveling everything in its path. "I think that you're right. But now, I have to figure out where my father may have left that information."

Just as I said the words, a car came down the long driveway leading from Mr. Harrington's mansion. I couldn't know with 100 percent certainty, but my guess was that Mr. Harrington was inside the Lincoln Town Car, neatly concealed behind the tinted windows.

Without saying anything else, Michael pulled out behind him.

This could all be for nothing.

But maybe not.

CHAPTER TWENTY

TWENTY MINUTES LATER, Mr. Harrington pulled up to one of his offices. The building wasn't exclusively his—there were other offices there as well. That fact increased our chance of getting inside.

We waited until Mr. Harrington was through the front door before following him. A quick glance at the building directory indicated his business office was located on the fourth floor. We took the elevator up. Granite walls and floors surrounded us, and the whole place felt fancy.

At the top, a bright-eyed, perky brunette receptionist greeted us with a wide grin from behind a gigantic wooden desk.

I tried to think quickly, to figure out a plan as to how Michael and I were going to get by her and find out where Mr. Harrington had gone.

My mind went blank, and I hoped that Michael had some ideas.

He seemed to. He put on his most charming smile and approached the desk. "Good morning."

The receptionist seemed to warm right up to him. Her professional smile suddenly turned into an all-out grin.

"Good morning. Why do I recognize you?" Her voice almost sounded flirty.

Michael shrugged. "Maybe from the Mets?"

Her eyes lit, and she snapped her fingers. "That's right. You're Michael Straley."

Michael leaned on the counter, using all the swagger he had inside him. "The one and only."

I might be jealous because he seemed to be flirting. But, in general, I wasn't the jealous type. Besides, I trusted Michael.

"What can I do for you, Michael?" The woman nearly sounded giddy as she asked the question and stared at him with stars in her eyes.

"I'm hoping I can talk to Mr. Harrington."

She froze for a second as if recalculating. "Are you here for his meeting?"

"Maybe." Now Michael was the one who sounded teasing and flirtatious.

The woman giggled. "Well, let me look at the list." She glanced at the paper in front of her and shrugged. "I'm sorry, but there is no Michael Straley on this list."

Michael leaned closer, as if trying to catch a glimpse of the paper. "Are you sure? Maybe it was an oversight."

"I'm afraid it's not an oversight." She shrugged, almost apologetically. "I wish I could help you. I'd put it on there myself if I could. But my hands are tied."

My shoulders slumped. Michael had given it his best shot. But we were going to need to think of something else.

As it turned out, we didn't need to think too hard.

Because somebody I knew walked in the door.

Someone I never expected to see here.

But I knew that this was no coincidence.

"ANDREA?" I turned to stare at Lily's mom.

Based on the way Andrea turned pale, she hadn't expected to see me here. She was wearing a navy-blue business suit and heels. Her designer purse was clutched beneath her arm, and a wrinkle of worry curled between her eyes.

"Elliot, right?" She froze, still gripping her purse.

"It's me. I wasn't expecting to see you here either."

She glanced beyond me, still looking like she was ready to spring. "Just here for a quick meeting. Any word on your sister?"

"No, nothing."

"I'm so sorry to hear that Ruth hasn't been located yet." Andrea's voice sounded thin as she frowned at me. "I was really hoping that wouldn't be the case."

"Mrs. Marino," the receptionist said behind us. "I'm sorry to interrupt, but Mr. Harrington's ready to see you now."

Andrea was part of the meeting.

I stored that information away, knowing that it would be helpful.

Michael and I watched as Andrea disappeared with a wave. There was nothing else we could do here.

Michael took my elbow and led me from the building.

"What do you think?" I asked quietly.

He rubbed his jaw as we strode through the lobby. "I think we'd be stupid to ignore this connection."

"So what next?"

Michael crossed his arms. "Now we wait for Andrea to leave, and we catch her alone to see what she'll tell us."

CHAPTER TWENTY-ONE

MICHAEL and I lingered near his minivan, waiting.

Last night's rain had turned into this morning's humidity. The sun bore down on us, creating sauna-like heat waves. A thin layer of sweat already spread across my skin.

As we waited, Michael's phone rang.

"It's Oscar," Michael said. "I'll put it on speaker."

"I lost him," Oscar muttered.

"Lost who?" A knot formed between Michael's eyes.

"Blaine. I've been out here for the past five hours. I thought he left so I followed. But the car that came from the garage had tinted windows, and I think it was actually Blaine's wife inside. By the time I realized that and got back to the house, the other car was gone from the garage also. I got out and looked in the window to double-check."

"It's okay," I told Oscar. "You did the best you could."

"It was a rookie mistake. It shouldn't have happened. Anyway, I'll wait here for a little bit longer to see if he comes back. I just wanted to say sorry." Oscar let out a sigh, sounding truly upset. "Any updates on your end?"

We told him what we'd learned.

As soon as we finished, Andrea emerged from the building. Her eyes widened when she saw us waiting for her, and she started walking in the opposite direction.

But we couldn't let that happen.

"Andrea!" I called, rushing after her.

She still didn't slow down.

I picked up my pace until I reached her side. "I've got to talk to you."

"I would," she called over her shoulder, still walking quickly. "I really would. But it's a bad day. I have a lot of appointments."

I grabbed her arm. She wasn't going to get out of it that easily. "I need to know what you know about my sister."

She froze and turned toward me, something about her gaze making me realize she was on edge.

"I wish I could help," she insisted, her hand fluttering through the air. "I really do."

Michael paused on the other side of Andrea. "You

know more than you're letting on. This girl's life is on the line. You have a daughter the same age as Ruth. How could you participate in something like this?"

Andrea's bottom lip dropped slightly. "I'm not participating in anything."

I also noticed that she didn't totally deny that she knew something.

I had to reach her somehow.

"Please." I softened my voice as I pleaded with her. "If this was your daughter—if it were Lily—you'd want someone to speak up for her."

She squeezed her eyes shut, her head bending toward the ground. I felt certain she was going to deny her involvement again. Instead, she let out a shaky breath.

"My husband is from South America," she announced.

I held my breath, waiting to hear what she had to say next.

Andrea rubbed her jaw, still looking uneasy. But she continued, "He said a good opportunity had come up, and he told Lily to invite Ruth to dinner, that the two of them should be friends."

My stomach squeezed as I realized the implications of what she said. This could be a lot worse than I'd imagined.

"What kind of opportunity did your husband say this was?" Michael rushed in before I could find the words.

Andrea's gaze met mine. "I don't know. He didn't tell me, and I didn't ask."

"What line of work is he in?" I continued, knowing this conversation was far from done.

"Ron works in investments. He doesn't really like to talk about what he does, and, quite honestly, I don't really care."

"But you suspected something was going on, didn't you?" I tried to keep the edge out of my voice, but it didn't work. If this woman had done something to put my sister in danger . . . then I had a hard time seeing where she deserved any grace right now.

"I don't know. I never dreamed that it would turn out like this, that Ruth would be missing. She was such a sweet girl. She *is* such a sweet girl," Andrea quickly corrected, her cheeks reddening.

I didn't miss the fact that she had used Ruth's name in past tense. My heart pounded harder, and my head felt lighter.

"Do you know where my sister is?" My voice hardened until I barely recognized it.

"I don't. I don't think my husband has anything to do with it. I promise."

"And what do you think is going on?" Michael squeezed in closer.

Andrea shrugged, her gaze shifting with uncertainty. "I don't know."

"What about your meeting with Mr. Harrington?" Michael asked. "Is that connected to this somehow?"

"I'm just helping him plan a fundraiser." Her voice turned no-nonsense as her hand sliced through the air. "That's it."

I wasn't so sure about that. But I was going to let it slide . . . for now. We'd gotten everything out of her that we could for the time being.

I CALLED Hunter and gave him the update. He promised to look into the situation with Andrea.

In the meantime, Michael and I had to figure out exactly what we were going to do next to find my sister. Every lead so far had led nowhere.

We decided to go back to the office. Velma was there, and I knew she would do everything she could to help me find answers. All I had to do was ask.

Right now, I needed them to look into the backgrounds of Andrea and her husband. Maybe there was something there that might offer a clue as to why they could have taken my sister.

I picked up a photo from my desk. A photo with Ruth.

She looked so happy in the snapshot. The Yerbian mountains were behind us. She wore a tank top, and her skin looked tanned and glowing. The two of us had our arms around each other as we smiled at the camera—as we smiled at my dad behind the camera.

I would have never guessed when that photo was taken two years ago where we'd be now.

If I could just go back and revisit that time . . .

"You okay?" Michael's voice pulled me from my memories.

I looked up at him and nodded, holding back my tears. What if I pulled Chloe and Michael into all this craziness? What if I put Chloe in a situation like I was in —one where she had only photos of her father to remember him by?

I could hardly stomach the thought.

Before I could get my thoughts together, my phone rang. It was Hunter.

I wondered if he had an update about Andrea so quickly.

I held my breath in anticipation after I answered.

"I have bad news," he started.

This wasn't a good start to the conversation. "What's going on?"

Michael scooted closer as if he wanted to hear also.

"It's about Blaine Kingsley. He was in a car accident this morning, and he didn't make it."

CHAPTER TWENTY-TWO

I SAT UP STRAIGHT. "What do you mean, Blaine was in an accident?"

Michael leaned even closer so he could hear what Hunter was saying.

"I'm at the scene right now," Hunter said. "It looks like he ran off the side of the road and hit a tree."

"And is he . . . dead?" My throat burned as I asked the question.

"There was no way anyone could have survived this crash. The whole car was on fire, and his body was burned nearly beyond recognition. I'm sorry, Elliot."

I pressed my eyes shut, trying to push out the pictures of the scene. "Was there any foul play involved?"

"We're still investigating it. As of right now, we only

see one set of skid marks. But we're just starting to figure things out here. Until we do, be extra careful."

I knew what Hunter was saying. He didn't think it was an accident. He couldn't be sure of it, at least.

Where had Blaine been heading? Was he about to share something that would have given us some answers? Had someone silenced him before he could do that?

It seemed like a good possibility.

I thanked Hunter for giving me the update and then ended the call and turned to Michael.

"I can't believe it either." Michael shook his head and looked off into the distance. "Someone wanted to keep Blaine quiet. Apparently, he knew more than he let on."

"There's only one person I can think of who might be guilty," I muttered. I almost didn't want to voice my thought aloud. But I knew I couldn't keep it silent either.

"Who is that?"

"Sergio." I stood and grabbed my purse. "I need to talk to him again. I need to know what he knows."

Michael grabbed my hand, stopping me. "Are you sure you want to do that?"

I didn't even have to think about it. "Absolutely."

"Then I'm going with you."

I wouldn't argue with that.

AS I STEPPED OUTSIDE, I nearly collided with someone coming toward the office.

Grayson.

Again.

"What are you doing here again?" I realized as the words left my lips that they might sound rude. That hadn't been what I had intended. My thoughts were just going so many different directions right now.

"Do you two have a minute?" Grayson stared at me then Michael.

Michael and I exchanged a nod. A few minutes later, the three of us were sitting in the office.

I didn't push Grayson to start. If Grayson came all the way here again, he obviously had something important that he wanted to say. Based on the sheen of sweat on his forehead, he was anxious.

"I had another memory," he finally started. "Again, it might not mean anything. But it could."

"What was it, Grayson?" I nearly sounded breathless as I asked the question.

"I remember smelling . . . doughnuts." Grayson shrugged.

I waited for him to say more, but he didn't.

"Like, your captors were eating doughnuts?" Michael asked, looking as confused as I felt.

"Not exactly." Grayson shifted, still looking incredibly

uncomfortable. "The smell was always there, if that makes sense."

"So you think they were holding you somewhere close to a doughnut shop?" I clarified, wanting to make sure I understood exactly what he was saying.

Grayson shrugged. "I guess that's what I mean. Like I said, I'm not sure it amounts to anything but—"

"Any information you remember is welcome right now," I said. "Thank you."

Relief seemed to wash through him as he nodded. He'd obviously been under a tremendous amount of stress lately. He didn't even seem like the same person I'd first met.

"Any updates on Ruth?" Grayson's eyes brightened, as if he hoped for good news.

I shook my head, wishing I could deliver—for my sake more than his. "No, unfortunately."

Grayson nodded stoically as he stood. "I really hope you find her, Elliot. I know you have to be beside yourself."

"To say the least," I said. "I'll let you know if we discover anything."

But now I really did need to talk to Sergio. There was no time to waste.

Then I would think about those doughnuts.

CHAPTER TWENTY-THREE

I PULLED up to Blaine's house and paused. I didn't want to be so focused on finding answers that I didn't take a moment to respect a life that had been lost.

Inside that house, Blaine's wife was in mourning. That wasn't to mention what a big loss this would be to the community.

"Are you sure you're okay with this?" Michael asked before we climbed from his minivan.

"I need answers. There's no way all of this isn't connected."

"I agree but . . . Blaine's wife may have just found out."

I sighed. "I know."

Just as I was contemplating what a bad idea this might be, the front door opened and Sergio stepped out.

Sergio? Was he staying with Blaine? That's what it seemed.

Either way, this was my chance to talk to him.

Before Michael could stop me, I darted across the sidewalk. "Sergio!"

He paused and stared at me.

"Elliot . . ." He stuffed his hands into the pockets of his designer pants as he waited for me.

"I'm so sorry about Blaine," I started.

His face seemed pale as he nodded. His gaze flickered behind me, probably to where Michael stood by his van. "Me too. We all are."

"I came right over when I heard." I casually rested my hands in the pockets of my jeans. "What happened? Do you know?"

"From what I understand, the roads were slick. He must have hit a puddle and lost control of his vehicle." He frowned, somber undertones clearly present in his voice. "It's such a tragedy."

"It really is. A huge loss for not only this area but for Yerba."

"Yes, it truly is." Sergio paused, as if waiting for me to continue.

I stepped closer, knowing I needed his total attention. "Sergio . . . have you thought of anything else?"

He froze a moment before raising his eyebrows. "About your sister?"

I nodded. "Yes, about Ruth."

"No, Elliot. I'm sorry. I haven't heard anything about her, nor do I know of anyone who might have taken her. I'm afraid this has no connection with Yerba. Perhaps she was dealing with some other problems here?"

"Sergio . . ." How could I get through to him? I almost wished it wasn't beyond me to want to beat the truth out of someone. But it was. And with my little muscles, it wouldn't do much good.

"I'm sorry, Elliot." Sergio frowned again. "But I must go."

My back straightened when I realized he was brushing me off. "Where are you hurrying off to?"

His gaze darkened. "I told you I wasn't in town just for pleasure. I have meetings to attend about Yerba."

"What about Mrs. Kingsley? You're just going to leave her alone?" I nodded toward the house.

Sergio stared at me as if I were confused. "I thought you knew that she's out of town. She'll return in the morning."

But if she was out of town, then who had pulled out of the Kingsley's garage and tricked Oscar? Had that been Sergio?

Unrest jostled in my chest.

I didn't know.

But I didn't like any of this.

I UPDATED Michael when I got back in the minivan. He grunted and made it clear what he thought about Sergio. Then he snapped right back into professional mode.

"You want to follow Sergio?" Michael asked.

It was an idea but . . . "Sergio is too smart to lead us anywhere. He'll lose us."

Michael shrugged, staring at the street ahead. "Maybe not."

I watched as Sergio pulled away. I didn't want to waste our time going that route.

After he disappeared from sight, Michael glanced at me. "What now?"

"I don't know." I let out a sigh, feeling my headache coming on again. "There hasn't been a ransom demand. That MamasBoy guy checked out—he isn't behind this. There were no other guys Ruth was talking to through that site. Where does that leave us, if not for Yerba?"

"I agree that this goes back to your father somehow."

I nibbled on my fingernail a minute as I thought everything through. "And what about what Grayson said? He remembers smelling doughnuts."

"I suppose it can't hurt to track down all the doughnut places in the area. Maybe it will trigger something."

I pulled out my phone and did a quick search. There were eight different places within a thirty-mile radius.

"We should get started, I guess," I said.

But I really hoped this led somewhere and wasn't just a royal waste of time.

CHAPTER TWENTY-FOUR

EIGHT DOUGHNUT STOPS LATER, Michael and I still had nothing.

None of the areas around the shops had triggered any clues or thoughts. To say I was bummed about that would be an understatement.

I was beginning to think this was all a waste of time— and time was a precious commodity right now.

Where was Ruth? Was she okay? I prayed she wasn't suffering. I prayed her place could be held for this transplant surgery.

But there were too many unknowns for my comfort right now.

As we headed back toward Storm River, Kitty called. She wanted to meet with us in an hour at my house to talk about the story she was doing on Ruth. I told her that was fine, but I called my mom to confirm. Mama also agreed that it was time to release the information publicly.

"We should probably get to my house early so I can talk to my mom and we can coordinate what we want to say before Kitty arrives," I told Michael.

"Sure thing."

We started that way, silence falling between us.

What a whirlwind this had been. In fact, my entire relationship with Michael had been a whirlwind.

But I was so glad to have him by my side throughout all of this.

I only prayed there would be a happy ending—not just for us but for this entire situation.

I also knew I was going to need to tell my mom what I knew. I couldn't risk her finding out from someone else, and time was running out.

There was no good opportunity or perfect time—so it might as well be now.

I need the right words to say because it's already been an awful day. But I feel so lost because I know the cost. But I can't be silent anymore because I knew I was fighting a war.

"ARE you sure you want to tell your mom everything?" Michael asked as we pulled up in front of my house and he put his minivan in Park.

I'd just told him about my plan. I figured I needed to say it aloud if I wanted to carry through with it. But even as I'd shared with him, nausea roiled in my stomach.

I nodded, even though I didn't feel sure at all. "It's the right thing. What if keeping this secret is somehow putting up a barrier to finding my sister? Maybe if my mom knows this information, we can begin to make sense of everything."

Michael's gaze lingered on me another moment until he finally nodded. "Okay then. I fully support your decision."

As we climbed out and walked toward my front door, my steps felt heavy. A flutter of nerves washed through me. I hoped this was the right thing. There were so many unknowns right now, though.

Before I even climbed the porch steps, the front door flew open.

"Anything?" My mom's eyes looked hopeful as she rushed toward Michael and me.

Even though we'd just talked on the way home and she probably already knew the answer, I still felt like I was letting her down when I said, "No. I'm sorry."

She nodded, as if she already knew that answer. Any

of the light that had been in her gaze disappeared. "Come on in."

She insisted on fixing us tea, and then the three of us sat in the living room, unspoken conversations hanging like an invisible noose around us. I knew I couldn't put this off anymore. I had to tell her what was going on.

"There's something I need to talk to you about, Mama," I finally started. My voice sounded more high-pitched than usual, and a slight tremble captured my vocal cords.

"What is it, dear?"

I nodded slowly. "I probably should have told you this a while ago. It's about Dad."

Her face tensed as she stared at me. "About your father? What about him?"

I licked my lips and sucked in a deep breath, wondering how to best say this. I decided to go with the blunt truth. "Mama, I'm afraid there are things he wasn't telling you. Really important things."

CHAPTER TWENTY-FIVE

MY MOM SET her cup of tea down on the coffee table as her eyes met mine. "You mean, like the fact your father was a spy?"

I blanched, certain I hadn't heard her correctly. "What?"

She nodded, her expression unchanged as she folded her hands in her lap. "I know, Elliot."

I shook my head, still uncertain what I'd heard. Only one minute in, and this conversation wasn't going anything like I'd expected it to. "He was a . . . what?"

"A spy."

I stared at my mom, still feeling speechless. She'd said the words like it was no surprise, like it was no big deal. But I'd been so certain she was clueless. "You knew?"

"Of course, I knew. Do you think your dad kept secrets from me?"

I leaned back on the couch, thankful for Michael's presence beside me. He took the tea from my hands and set it on the table. I'd only half realized that the cup had been shaking in my hands. Not even the scent of lavender would help me calm down right now.

"He kept it a secret from the family," I reminded her.

"He couldn't risk you girls knowing," Mama said, absently fluffing a beige pillow beside her. "You would have been in too much danger."

"But . . ." I still couldn't comprehend this. I'd been certain that my mom was clueless, that my father had kept it from her and let her continue on blissfully as she ministered to children in the area. She was a Bible-toting, Jesus-loving, peace-seeking Christian woman.

This did not fit. Not at all.

"I'm sorry we kept it from you, Elliot," she continued. "But his position was classified."

"What else do you know?" I shifted, not really sure if I wanted to hear her answer or not. My whole world felt like it had been thrown off balance right now. How many times could this happen in a person's lifetime? In a person's year, for that matter?

She leaned forward and squeezed my hand. "It's complicated, dear."

That wasn't going to cut it. Not considering everything that had happened and everything I'd been through.

"What about his death?" I stared at her, trying to test the waters. I didn't know if Mama had any suspicions that his death hadn't been natural, and I wasn't sure I wanted to plant them.

"I've often wondered if there was more to it than we thought." Her voice cracked, and she rubbed her throat, her eyes becoming misty again.

I shook my head. "Mama..."

I didn't know what else to say. I'd expected to be the one breaking this news to her. But knowing that she knew ... it made my head pound.

"I'm sorry, Elliot. But your father knew things about the uprising. That's why we had to get out of Yerba. People wanted him dead."

"So they killed him here in the States instead?" My throat burned as I said the words.

She swallowed hard and glanced down at her lap. "Yes. Of course, we'd hoped that wouldn't be the outcome. But it appeared that our enemies followed us."

I couldn't believe she'd kept all of this quiet. "Mama .. . what if these enemies have Ruth now?"

My mom's tear-filled eyes met mine. "Don't think I haven't thought about it."

"Then why didn't you say anything?" None of this was making sense to me.

"I didn't want to make things harder on you."

I opened my mouth. I wanted to argue, but her reasoning was the same as mine.

We'd both been trying to protect each other.

How could I be mad about that?

Michael shifted beside us. "Mrs. Ransom, is there anything you know that might help us find Ruth?"

Mama let out a sigh. "All I know is this. Your father constantly said that he followed the money. That's what led him to finding the answers he did. I just have to wonder where that money leads now."

"What money?" I held my breath as I waited for the answer.

"The money Xavier Flores used to overthrow the government."

WHEN HUNTER and Kitty showed up, I was still dwelling on what Mama had told me.

I couldn't believe she knew. I couldn't believe she'd kept it from me.

Then again, maybe I could since I'd done the same.

But we'd been dancing around the fire like we didn't have a guinea pig to roast for so long. How much time and energy would we have saved if we'd both opened up?

It was too late to think about that now.

Now I needed to figure out how to follow the money. I didn't even know where to start.

We all sat around the kitchen table together, but I only half listened to the conversation taking place. Mama and Hunter were giving Kitty all the pertinent details, and I tried to nod on occasion.

I didn't want to be here. I didn't want this to be real. I wanted to wake up and discover this was all a bad dream.

But it wasn't.

"I hope we can trust you with this information," Hunter told Kitty.

"Of course you can," Kitty said. "Have I ever let you down before?"

Hunter didn't say anything. Instead, the two stared at each other from across the table.

Finally, Hunter looked back at my mom and me. "The Amber Alert should be going out in an hour. I'm hoping we'll get some good leads from it."

I nodded. "Thank you."

"And I'll get started on the article," Kitty added. "Maybe someone will come forward with some information. I know you're anxious to find your sister—anyone in your shoes would be."

"We appreciate it." My voice cracked. This still seemed surreal. But this article and the Amber Alert were the next logical steps. Maybe by making what had happened public, we could find answers.

Hunter's gaze met mine. "Could I talk to you a minute, Elliot?"

"Of course." But the tone of his voice set me on edge.

We stepped outside, and I braced myself for whatever he was about to say. If this conversation had to take place in private, then it probably wasn't good.

"I looked into Andrea, just like you asked me to," he started. "Her husband, Ron, is from Peru, and his company has some interesting ties with Peter Harrington."

"What does that mean?" I wasn't sure what he was getting at, but I was dying to know.

He narrowed his eyes and shrugged. "Honestly, I'm not sure it necessarily means anything. Or it could mean everything. We have to do some more digging."

"What if Andrea knows where Ruth is?" I rushed.

Hunter frowned. "I've already talked to them, Elliot. They volunteered to let me search their home. We found nothing there. But we're not giving up. We're going to keep digging. We're going to find answers somehow or another."

I tried to smile to show my appreciation. But I also felt my shoulders slump.

One step closer and two steps back.

That seemed to be the story of my life.

CHAPTER TWENTY-SIX

"HOW DO WE FOLLOW THE MONEY?" I asked Michael thirty minutes later. That thought hadn't left my mind since my mom shared it.

We sat in his minivan. Hunter had returned to work. Linda had arrived to stay with my mom. And Kitty was hard at work on her article, I presumed.

Now we needed to get back to work also.

The sun beat down on us, despite the blast from the AC in front of us. Hot weather had moved in, promising a scorching summer.

Normal people around here planned days on their boats or on the sandy riverside beach.

I wished I'd been afforded those choices.

Michael leaned back and crossed his arms. "I'm not even sure what money we're following."

"Me either."

I frowned, realizing we weren't getting anywhere. "I can't even ask Blaine anymore—God rest his soul—and I'm sure Sergio wouldn't be forthcoming with the information."

Michael stared off into the distance at two kids riding their bikes on the sidewalk and shook his head. "Let's think here. There has to be something we're missing. But what?"

There was only one thing I could think of. "Doesn't all of this go back to money and power? Isn't that why Xavier wanted to take control of the country?"

"It seems to fit the narrative. But how does knowing that help us find answers?"

"Where does Xavier get his money? He grew up poor, which was how he lured people into relating to him," I said. "As soon as he came into power, he began living a lux lifestyle. But the people have no money. Businesses have dried up. Even if he doubled people's taxes, he still wouldn't amass so much wealth."

Michael shifted to face me. "So what's your theory?"

"Maybe he makes money by making deals with other governments or other people from the outside."

His eyebrows popped up. "Like Mr. Harrington?"

I nodded. "Yes, like Mr. Harrington."

"But what would be in it for Mr. Harrington?"

"I'm . . . I'm not sure."

"We obviously need to flesh it out some more."

My mind continued to race. "What if my dad found out about this? It can't be legal."

"And if he had a list of names of those involved . . . it would be reason enough for someone to want to kill you."

I let that thought settle over me.

I didn't like where this was going.

But at least we were getting closer to finding some answers.

Now I wanted to talk to Andrea Marino again.

"TELL me why you were really meeting with Mr. Harrington." I stared Andrea down, tired of playing games.

She'd just answered the door, and I hadn't wasted any time asking my questions.

There was no time to waste here.

She stood in the door, still in her business attire, and blinked rapidly as if I'd taken her by surprise.

Good.

I hadn't wanted to give her a heads-up.

"I don't know what you're getting at," she finally said. One of her hands gripped the door, as if she might slam it at any minute.

"But you obviously do," I said. "I can't believe you're

allowing these lies to continue. My sister and your daughter were friends."

Her face hardened. "I'm so sorry for what's happened to you. But it's like I told you, I don't know what you're talking about. I have no idea where Ruth is."

"Please, ma'am." Michael stepped forward, his voice even and more composed than mine. "This is a matter of life or death."

Andrea stared at us a moment, and I thought she might crack. Then, the next instant, she drew her shoulders up and shrugged. "I really do wish I could help. I'm sorry. I hope you find your sister. I even let the police search my home. I don't have anything to do with her disappearance."

"But—" I started.

Before I could finish my question, Andrea closed the door and the lock clicked into place.

So much for that lead.

Michael turned to me as we stood there on the stoop. "It was worth a try."

But had it been? It seemed like a waste of time.

Michael squeezed my shoulder. "We're going to find answers, Elliot."

"Too much time is passing." I shook my head. "The further we get away from the time Ruth went missing, the less likely we are to find her."

"Don't give up hope." He nudged my chin up until my eyes met his.

"I feel like I'm trying to race through a mud pit but not going anywhere." It was a Yerbian expression.

"You mean you're spinning your tires?"

I narrowed my gaze. "What sense does that make?"

Michael shook his head. "It doesn't matter. Either way, we're moving slowly, but we're going to find answers."

I tried to smile. "Thanks for the encouragement."

We walked back to his minivan and climbed inside.

Just as Michael cranked the engine, a shadow appeared at my window.

I sucked in a breath when I saw who was there.

CHAPTER TWENTY-SEVEN

"LILY?"

She glanced over the minivan at her house. "Can I get in?"

"I'm not sure that's a good idea," Michael muttered.

"Please, I need to talk to you," she said.

Michael and I exchanged a look.

"Get in," Michael finally said. "But make it quick."

Lily climbed in the back seat, her chest rising and falling with adrenaline. "I can't let my mom or dad see me."

"Great . . ." Michael muttered.

I turned to face her better, my only concern finding my sister. "What's going on, Lily?"

"I'm so sorry about Ruth." Her chin trembled as she

leaned between our seats. "I've been so worried about her."

"Do you know something that could help us find her?" I held my breath as I waited for her answer. Was this the break we'd been waiting for?

"I . . . I don't know." She rubbed a hand over her face, her inner turmoil obvious.

"We know your dad encouraged you to become friends with her," I prodded, trying to make this easier for her.

"But our friendship was real." Tears glimmered in Lily's eyes. "I promise, it was."

"I believe you, Lily." I studied her face. "Do you have any idea where she might be right now? We have to find her."

"I just know my mom and dad have been whispering a lot lately. I don't know what's going on with them."

"You have no clue?" Michael clarified.

Lily let out a long breath. "I heard them saying something about starting a new company."

I stored that information in the back of my mind. Andrea hadn't mentioned any new company when I had talked to her earlier. Could this have something to do with what was going on in Yerba? I wasn't putting the pieces together yet.

"You have no idea what kind of company this is?" I clarified.

"No, but whatever it is it must be stressful." Lily shook her head. "I do know that my mom has been looking at new houses. Bigger houses. Houses on the water."

So whatever this investment was, Andrea must stand to get a good payoff out of it.

This had to have something to do with her meeting with Mr. Harrington. And I was nearly certain it also connected with Yerba.

The problem was, how did we prove any of it?

I didn't have the answer to that question.

"OSCAR IS GOING to try to find out what kind of company it is that Andrea set up," Michael announced a few minutes later as he lowered his phone to his lap.

Lily had climbed from the minivan and run back to her house, leaving Michael and me to discuss what she'd told us.

"Maybe if he can figure that out, then we can figure out what's going on here." I pressed my lips together, desperately wanting answers more quickly than we were getting them. "I feel nearly certain that Mr. Harrington has something to do with this."

Michael nodded slowly. "I think you're right."

"But I'm not sure that tells us how to find my sister

either." I nibbled on my bottom lip as I tried to think it all through.

"If Mr. Harrington is involved here, then he's working with people from Yerba to secure these funds. It's probably these people from Yerba who have taken your sister."

I didn't like the sound of that. "Why don't we try to go back to Shipwrecks again and see if anybody is there?"

"I think that's a great idea. With any luck, we'll see somebody who has some answers. We can follow them, see where they go."

It was worth a shot. And it was all we had right now.

I just hoped that this outing led us to some results and not another dead-end.

CHAPTER TWENTY-EIGHT

SHIPWRECKS LOOKED the same as it did last time Michael and I were here. The only difference was that there were a lot more customers today, including a group of three men who gathered at one of the tables across the room. Men with tanned skin and dark hair. Men who looked like they could be from my home country of Yerba.

Before we'd come inside, Michael had given me a hat. I pulled the baseball cap low over my face, just in case anybody recognized me as we walked in. A few minutes later, Michael and I were seated two tables over from the men—close enough to possibly overhear what they were saying but not so close as to draw attention.

We ordered some sweet tea and crab cake sandwiches. As we waited for our order, I tuned my ears to the conversation. The men mostly seemed to be blowing off steam, talking about the weather, boating, and sporting events. Nothing that offered many answers.

Our food was delivered, and I was halfway through my sandwich before I overheard anything interesting.

One of the men said the name Sergio.

Michael and I exchanged a glance.

I leaned closer, trying to figure out what they were saying about my ex-fiancé.

"The new president is grooming him," one of the men said.

My spine stiffened. Had I heard that correctly? Was Sergio really being groomed to take over the top position in Yerba?

If that was the case, then he would have a lot at stake here. In fact, he might be desperate and willing to do whatever was necessary in order to come into power.

Could Sergio be the one behind all of this? Did my father have information on him that could bring him down? Even worse—could my ex-fiancé have been involved in my father's death?

I didn't know. But the questions were unsettling, to say the least.

Right now I needed these guys to say something about my sister. Could one of these men have taken her? Did they have the answers I desperately sought?

I stared at them from beneath the brim of the hat. I

didn't recognize any of the men. But that didn't mean that one of them hadn't been keeping an eye on me.

Either way, none of them had glanced my way when I walked in. Did that mean they didn't recognize me? Or were they just terrible operatives who didn't pay attention?

I didn't know.

When the conversation went back to sports again, I decided I needed a breather. My adrenaline had been pumping, and now my hopes began to deflate.

"I'm going to run to the restroom," I told Michael.

Keeping my head low, I hurried down the hallway in the distance. I escaped into a stall and took some deep breaths, savoring having a moment to catch my breath and compose myself. I was tired. Angry. Worried.

At any minute, I might completely fall apart.

Then I wouldn't be any good to anyone.

I sucked in a few more deep breaths before opening the door to the stall. I needed to get back out there to Michael.

But before I could step out into the bathroom common area, the room went dark.

Great. Had somebody accidentally hit the switch? Were the lights on a timer?

The red glow from an Exit sign above the door offered a little light.

And illuminated something across the room.

A person.

Dressed like a chicken.

Dread pooled in my stomach.

What kind of threats did he hold for me this time?

"WHAT DO YOU WANT?" My voice trembled as I asked the question.

I took a step back, wanting to put as much space as I could between me and this man. But there was nowhere else to go. The man blocked the door.

"All I want is the information," he crooned.

"And I told you that I don't have the information."

"I beg to differ, Elliot Ransom. You just need to search a bit harder."

What kind of game was this guy playing? Either way, I needed to turn the tables. This was my best chance to get information from him. "You took my sister, didn't you?"

He lowered his voice. "I told you that drastic measures would be taken if you did not comply."

"You didn't even give me a chance to comply before you kidnapped her." Anger seeped into my words as they left my lips. This man was the lowest of the low.

"I needed for you to know that I was serious."

"I'm well aware of that fact," I growled. "Let Ruth go. Take me instead."

"If I have you then you cannot find that information, can you?" He said the words casually, like this was an everyday situation instead of a life-threatening one.

Despair pressed down on me, and I wanted to cry out.

Almost as if the man could read my mind, he said, "If you make a scene, all I have to do is make one phone call and your sister is dead. So do not even think about it."

I tamped down the scream that wanted to emerge. I couldn't do anything to put my sister at risk. Chicken Man clearly knew that.

"You have twenty-four hours," the man said. "I think we have given you ample time."

"Twenty-four hours?" I nearly screeched. "That's not nearly enough time. Especially since I don't even know what I'm looking for."

"You need to figure it out. You are a smart woman. You can do this."

"Please," I begged him. "Just let my sister go. Please."

I wished I could see the man's face. I wanted to see his eyes. But it was no use. All I could see was that stupid chicken mask.

"I am sorry," was the last thing I remembered him saying.

Then he sprayed something in my face, and everything went black . . . again.

CHAPTER TWENTY-NINE

"ELLIOT?" Someone shook me.

I pulled my eyes open and saw Michael leaning over me.

Everything rushed back.

The man in the chicken costume.

Here.

In the bathroom.

He'd sprayed me with that substance again, and everything had gone black.

I jerked my head around, looking for any sign of him.

I saw none. Just bathroom stalls. Two lone sinks. A yellowing floor with dirty baseboards.

"It's okay." Michael tugged my shoulders until I sat up, leaning against him. "No one else is here."

It was almost like Michael could read my thoughts. He must have put things together and realized what had happened.

I ran a hand through my hair, realizing that my baseball cap had fallen off.

Then a new thought slapped me in the face.

"He was just here," I muttered, my gaze locking with Michael's. "Maybe you can—"

"He's gone." Michael's voice nearly sounded apologetic. "You were only in the bathroom five minutes. By the time I came to check on you, there was no sign of the man who did this to you."

I let out a long breath, one laced with a groan. I should have done something differently, but I wasn't sure what. I'd had the opportunity to get answers, and I'd failed.

Again.

Just like I was failing my sister now.

"I don't know how he got in here and got away without anyone seeing him," I muttered. How did someone sneak around in a chicken costume without being spotted?

"That's the kind of man he is. He must have gone out the back way."

"Maybe we can talk to some of the kitchen staff." Excitement hitched my voice. "Maybe they saw his face."

"We can, but I wouldn't get your hopes up." Michael frowned, his eyes still assessing me for damage or signs of injury. "This guy is slick. What did he say to you?"

I pulled myself fully up, my head throbbing. I must have hit it when I collapsed onto the tile floor.

"He said that we had only twenty-four hours to find this information or Ruth would . . ." I couldn't finish the sentence. The words caught in my throat until a garbled cry escaped.

"We're going to find her." Michael squeezed my shoulder. "Don't give up hope now."

"Maybe I should go out there right now and confront these guys," I said, desperation controlling my voice. "Certainly they know something."

"I doubt they're going to tell you any of it."

I pulled myself to my feet. "It's worth a shot. I don't have anything else to lose at this point."

Before Michael could stop me, I charged out from the restroom. But I paused when I reached the dining area.

The men were gone.

It almost looked like they'd never been here.

It appeared I'd missed the opportunity to find out any information from them.

More failure pressed on me.

"THERE HAS to be something we're missing," I told Michael as we stood outside the restaurant.

Michael stared in the distance before rubbing his jaw in thought. "Maybe we should go through everything you brought here from Yerba, just to make sure there's nothing that's been missed."

I frowned, knowing where he was coming from but wanting to do something more active. I wanted answers, and desperation was beginning to set in. All this passive research only made my head pound.

"I'm not opposed to doing that, I'm just afraid it will be a royal waste of time," I finally said. "And time isn't something that we have."

"What about that jewelry box?" Michael said. "That's what my thoughts keep going back to. Could there be something else hidden there?"

"After I found the first hidden compartment, I looked all over for anything else that might be concealed. I didn't find it. But you're right. It might be worth taking another look." At least it was something, I supposed.

With that settled, Michael and I started back toward my house. As we pulled away, my phone beeped. I looked down and saw that the Amber Alert about Ruth had gone out.

Seeing it further drove home the reality of our situation.

I could only hope that maybe somebody had seen something and would come forward with information.

But for now, I would continue to search for whatever it was these men wanted.

———————

WHEN MICHAEL and I walked into my house, I spotted my mom sitting on the couch with her phone to her ear. I imagined she'd be getting a lot of phone calls right now since the Amber Alert had gone out.

Since she seemed preoccupied, Michael and I waved to her before escaping back to my room. This might be the perfect opportunity to look at the jewelry box— though I was trying not to get my hopes up that we'd find anything.

We sat on the edge of my bed, and I picked up the wooden box my father had made me when we first came to this country. It was carved out of rich mahogany, had a door on each side, and various drawers at the center.

I thought the gift was strange since I hardly wore any jewelry. But I still loved the fact that my father had been thinking of me.

One day, when I had been looking at it, I'd accidentally pulled down on one of the hooks where necklaces could hang. When I did, a hidden compartment at the bottom of the wooden box popped out. That's where I found the journal that my father left me.

I wished the journal was the clue I'd been looking for. However, there hadn't been any high stakes information there. It was mostly just advice that my father had left me.

Michael sat across from me on the bed to examine it. "Where did you get this jewelry that's inside?"

"Most of it is just cheap stuff I brought with me from Yerba. Nothing is valuable."

"Is there anything new? Did any of this come from your dad?"

"Those fake diamond earrings and the matching necklace were from my dad. But I seriously doubt there's information hiding there."

Michael picked up one of the earrings and held it to the sunlight. "It looks normal."

"When he gave them to me, he told me he wished they were real diamonds, but that he couldn't afford that right now. Maybe one day."

It didn't bother me. I wasn't the diamond earring type of girl.

Michael lowered the earrings back into their case before examining the rest of the jewelry.

Once he went through everything and pulled on every hook and tugged on every drawer, he let out a sigh.

He hadn't found anything either.

Oh well. It had been worth a shot.

"Looks like we're back to the drawing board, as you Americans like to say." I leaned back against my headboard.

Michael's gaze met mine. "This jewelry box is the only thing that makes sense, Elliot."

"But you and I have both been through it. There's nothing there."

Michael picked up those earrings again and studied them another moment. "I keep thinking it goes back to this jewelry your dad gave you."

"But how?" I asked. "The earrings are so small. What could possibly be hiding on them?"

"I don't know." He picked up the matching necklace, which had a small pendant at the end. "How attached to them are you?"

My eyes widened when I heard the catch in his voice. "What are you suggesting?"

"I want to take them apart."

"Really?" I had no idea what that might prove.

Michael stared at me. "It could be nothing. I don't want to be totally off base with this theory and crush your heart in the process."

"I'm not overly attached to anything. If that's what we have to do to find answers then . . . I suppose that's what we have to do."

Michael stared at me another moment, studying my

gaze as if trying to determine if I told the truth. "Are you sure?"

I hesitated only a second before nodding. "I'm sure. Let's do it."

CHAPTER THIRTY

I HELD my breath as I watched Michael raise a painted rock that I normally used as a doorstop. My necklace rested atop a pillowcase cover I'd put on the wooden floor.

Michael brought the rock down on top of the pendant.

The fake precious gem shattered into pieces.

I expected just to see broken rock fragments on the floor.

But my breath caught when I saw something else there as well.

Carefully, Michael reached down and picked up what almost looked like a memory chip.

The black device was square and maybe one

centimeter wide with tiny prongs on the side. It had been located in the center of the pendant, well out of sight.

My gaze caught Michael's.

"Do you think that's it?" The words burned as they left my lips.

He held it closer to examine it more. "I think this is it, Elliot. This is what we've been looking for. We were right. The answers were hiding in plain sight the whole time, we just couldn't see it."

I should have known that my dad would do something like this. Who would have ever thought to look inside a cheap necklace? No one—except my dad.

"What now?" I asked.

"Now we need to find out what's on this."

"Grayson," I muttered. "He's the only one I know who might be able to figure it out for us. But do we really want to put him in that position again?"

"Good question." Michael frowned. "I'm not sure if we have any other choice."

I thought about it for a long moment. I supposed that Grayson could say no if he was really uncomfortable with it. Or maybe he could even tell us how to unlock this information. Either way, we had to talk to him.

"Is he still working from home right now?" I asked Michael.

"He is."

"Let's go pay him a visit."

JUST AS WE pulled up to Grayson's apartment building, we saw his red sports car pull out of the parking garage. Neither Michael nor I needed to say anything. Michael simply began to follow him.

I supposed we could have waited or come back later. But I really wanted to talk to Grayson now. With any luck, he was just doing a coffee run and we could catch him for a few minutes at a nearby shop.

Either way, that memory chip seemed to burn a hole in my pocket. I couldn't wait to find out what might be on it.

We continued to follow Grayson as he wove in and out of traffic. It almost appeared that he was heading toward Storm River. Was he coming to see us?

I had no idea.

But right now, it felt like the man was never going to stop. I heard the mental timer ticking away in my head. I had to get this memory chip to him, and I needed to get it to him quickly. Ruth had no time to waste.

I could call him. But something internal stopped me from doing that. I didn't want to put this information over the airwaves. Besides, Grayson was afraid that his phone and/or apartment could still be bugged.

I didn't want to take any chances.

Finally, Grayson pulled to a stop in front of a blue

house in a suburban neighborhood. It was a two-story structure with a neatly manicured lawn, typical of Storm River.

No other cars were at the house. That didn't stop Grayson. He hurried to the door and slipped inside, almost as if he owned the place.

"Interesting," I muttered.

"Maybe he has a key to this place," Michael said.

But I could hear some skepticism in his voice as well.

Just whose place was this?

Michael stopped on the opposite corner where we could still see the house—and Grayson if he came back outside. But it shouldn't be entirely obvious that the two of us were staking this place out either.

Something just wasn't making sense to me. "I don't get it. This isn't Grayson's place, unless he has some type of rental property or something. Did he ever mention that to you?"

Michael shook his head. "He didn't—although why would he?"

"That's the only explanation that makes sense. If he owns this place and he's checking on it."

"That would explain how he had gotten in so easily," Michael conceded.

"Should we go talk to him?" I asked.

Michael's jaw flexed, and he shook his head. "Not yet. It would be too weird if we showed up right now."

I was inclined to agree with him.

I just needed to be patient.

A few minutes later, another car pulled into the driveway.

I sat up straighter, my full attention on the scene.

Especially when I saw who stepped out of the car.

I sucked in a breath.

Sergio.

What was he doing here? And how did he know Grayson?

CHAPTER THIRTY-ONE

"I'VE GOT to see what's going on in that house." I reached for the door handle.

Before I could open it, Michael grabbed my arm. "What are you thinking about doing? You can't just charge up there. You could get yourself killed, at worst, or show your hand too quickly, at best."

His words made sense, but my logic wasn't kicking in right now. My emotions fueled my reactions, and I was too wound up to try to stop them. "I don't have time to play these games anymore."

Michael raised his hand as if trying to calm me. "I know that. But maybe there's a better way to go about this."

I took a deep breath, trying to even out my thoughts. I

should listen to Michael right now. He was more level-headed. "And what would that be?"

Michael glanced back at the house and frowned. "Let's listen to what they're saying. Let's practice a little bit of that art of eavesdropping I taught you when you first started with Driscoll and Associates."

I let his idea settle over me and agreed that it seemed like the best choice. Because why in the world would I think that either Grayson or Sergio would be forthcoming about their meeting? They wouldn't be. They would just feed me lies.

Michael and I climbed from his van and hurried across the street. Thankfully, the street was lined with trees and cars that helped conceal us as we approached the house. The last thing we wanted was to draw more attention to ourselves or for a neighbor to report us as suspicious.

A privacy fence surrounded the structure. We would need to get over that if we wanted to get close enough to hear what was going on inside.

Michael boosted me up, and I managed to practically fall to the other side of the fence.

As soon as I hit the ground, I sucked in a breath.

A dog rushed toward me.

A nice dog or mean dog? I couldn't be sure.

When I heard the dog let out a low growl, all my muscles tightened. What was I going to do?

The next instant, Michael appeared beside me—except he landed on his feet, kind of like a cat instead of a sack of potatoes.

He helped me stand before pulling something from his pocket and unwrapping it. It was some beef jerky he'd been munching on earlier. Michael held it out to the dog.

The golden-coated canine with floppy ears slowed its steps and sniffed the air.

A moment later, the dog took the treat from Michael, happily chewing it as it sat in front of us. When finished, the dog looked up at Michael, as if begging for more.

Michael leaned forward and patted the dog on its head. The canine leaned into his touch and began wagging its tail. After our new friendship was forged, Michael and I moved closer to the house. The dog followed as if curious.

When I reached the wood siding near a window, I realized I was too short to see inside.

I found a bucket, turned it over, and propped myself up on it. It should give me just enough height.

My fingers gripped the wooden windowsill as I pulled myself up. When I peered into the room, I could see that this window was near the kitchen. But just beyond that room was the living room.

And that was where Grayson and Sergio stood talking.

I desperately wanted to know what they were discussing.

"We need to go to the other side of the house," I whispered. "I need to know what they're saying."

Michael didn't ask any questions. We grabbed the bucket then started across the lawn. For once, I was grateful that the fence concealed us from anybody on the outside.

Meanwhile, the dog trotted along happily beside us.

I reached the area near the living room. But instead of standing on the bucket where I might be seen, Michael and I pressed ourselves near the window.

Then we listened.

"I need that information," Sergio said. "You were supposed to get it for us."

"I've been trying. Elliot hasn't given anything to me."

"You're one of the few people she trusts," Sergio said. "You know what's at stake here."

"I'm doing my best." Grayson's voice sounded thin.

I let that sink in. Grayson was working for these guys? This whole time I'd trusted him and . . . he wasn't even on my side?

Michael and I exchanged glances, and I could see the anger wash through Michael's eyes also.

"You have twenty-four hours," Sergio continued. "We're not playing nice. We have given you every opportunity to carry through with this."

"But . . ."

Before Grayson could even finish that statement, foot-steps pounded across the floor.

Sergio was leaving, I realized.

Michael and I needed to hide before he saw us.

JUST AS I heard the front door open, another sound floated from the backyard.

Michael and I ducked behind a bush.

"Samson!" Grayson called.

Samson must be the dog's name. But the canine hadn't walked inside with Grayson when he'd arrived here thirty minutes ago. Certainly, Grayson didn't leave the dog here by himself all the time.

I knew I had bigger worries at the moment, but I loved it when things made sense. It brought me a small measure of comfort when pieces fit together.

The front door closed, and I heard footsteps cross the porch. I couldn't see over the fence separating the front yard from the back, but I pictured Sergio walking toward his car. A moment later, an engine started.

It sounded like the man was leaving.

Meanwhile, Samson appeared to have gone into the house with Grayson.

Just like Michael and I needed to do.

Neither of us had to say anything to each other. Michael took my hand and pulled me along the house until he reached the back door. We hunched low as we climbed the steps. Without knocking, Michael opened the door, and we stepped inside.

Grayson turned from where he stood in the hallway, and his eyes widened when he spotted us. Just as quickly as his surprise appeared, so did his disappointment. His shoulders slumped, and he shook his head, almost appearing defeated.

"I trusted you." Michael stormed toward him. "How could you do this to us?"

"It's not like you think it is." Grayson raised his hands in defense, as if pleading for Michael and me to slow our thoughts.

Michael crossed his muscular arms over his chest. "Then what is it like? Because I thought you were my friend, and now you're meeting with Sergio Sanchez."

I stepped closer, anxious to hear what Grayson had to say.

But first I had to make certain of something.

I hurried to the front window. Just as I peered out, I saw Sergio's car disappear down the road.

He was gone.

That was a good thing because Michael, Grayson, and I had some serious conversations to have here.

CHAPTER THIRTY-TWO

"YOU NEED to tell us what's going on," Michael growled.

I joined them again and gave Grayson a hard stare as I waited for his response. I didn't take well to betrayal, and I'd never seen this one coming.

"It's not what you think," Grayson insisted. He raised his hands and took a step back. Beside him, Samson whined, as if the dog knew something was wrong.

"What I think is that you're working for the other side," Michael said.

I wasn't sure I'd ever seen him look so upset or angry. But I couldn't blame him. Grayson had been his friend, a person he'd trusted. How could he have done this?

"It's not like that." Grayson ran his hands through his short hair. He glanced around again before walking to the sink and turning the water on. "Just in case."

I knew what he was hinting at. *Just in case anybody had bugged this place.*

Or was this all an act? Was he going through the motions to make us believe he might still be a victim here?

"I haven't been entirely truthful with you," he started, his voice low. "But not by my own free will."

"Either you're working for them or you're not," Michael said. "Which one is it?"

Grayson sagged against the counter, his face about three shades lighter than it normally was. "Those men really did grab me and take that jump drive. They tried to force me to crack the code and get into it."

"And?" I tapped my foot against the floor, hardly able to wait to hear his answer. I despised it when people lied to me.

He ran a hand over his face. "Truthfully? I was able to break into that jump drive."

"And?" I held my breath, hardly able to wait one more second.

"There was nothing there. It was empty."

My lungs seemed to deflate at the news.

However, that had been Michael's theory. It looked like he was right—that is, if Grayson was telling the truth.

"Then what?" Michael pushed.

"Unlike what I told you, I didn't escape from those men," Grayson continued. "They let me go. They told me that I needed to find out the information from you, Elliot. They took my sister, and they're holding her captive until I do what they say."

My stomach sank at his words. Based on Grayson's body language, he told the truth. And, if that was the case, I knew exactly what he was feeling right now. "When did they take her?"

"It's been a week." He ran a hand through his hair, his eyes hollow. "I didn't think they would carry through with their threat, but they did. That's when I knew I had to try to get that information from you. Her life depends on it."

"I don't have that information, Grayson," I reminded him.

"That's what I keep trying to tell them, but they don't believe me." His face pinched, and he looked like he might cry.

I shook my head, trying to let all of this sink in. I hadn't expected any of this, not by any stretch of the imagination.

"What's your sister's name?" I asked.

"Sarah. She's twenty-three. This is her place."

I glanced around, turning my thoughts from those new facts to something with more definitive answers. "Why did you come here?"

Grayson glanced around. "This is my sister's dog, Samson. I come over a few times a day to check on him. These guys told me if I reported Sarah missing that they'd hurt her. I told all of Sarah's friends that she went away on a vacation, and I'm dog-sitting."

I supposed that made sense. But this situation just kept getting worse and worse.

I crossed my arms, part of me still feeling betrayed by his deceit. "Tell me what Sergio's role is in all of this."

Grayson's gaze darkened at the mention of the man's name. "This is only the second time I've met with him. He's desperate to get his hands on that information."

So Sergio *was* somehow involved with this? He probably even knew where Ruth was being held.

A new round of anger rose up in me. I couldn't believe that jerk would put my sister at risk.

Did he know that my father had been murdered, for that matter?

Another round of red-hot fury boiled through my blood.

If I got my hands on Sergio right now, I didn't know what exactly I would do to the man. But I knew everything in me wanted to strangle him, revive him, and then do it again.

It wasn't my normal, peace-loving MO. But I'd never felt a rage like this either.

I stared at Grayson another moment.

Could I trust this man? Was he telling us the truth? Or was this just another ruse?

I still had that chip in my pocket. He was the only person I knew who might be able to crack it.

But I wasn't sure telling him about it was worth the risk.

Because in his desperation to save his sister, he might compromise the only piece of leverage I had.

"MICHAEL, CAN WE TALK?" I finally said as I tried to sort out my thoughts.

"Of course." Michael gave Grayson a warning glance. "You can't go anywhere."

Grayson shrugged. "There's nowhere I can go where these guys can't find me."

"I'm serious." Michael's tone didn't cut him any slack. "This conversation isn't done."

"I'm serious too. These guys have my sister. I'm not going to do anything to put Sarah's life in danger."

I started to step toward the back door but paused. My question may seem random but I wanted to know. "When you told me that you smelled doughnuts when you were taken captive . . . were you telling the truth?"

Grayson nodded. "I was hoping that clue might lead you somewhere. That you may be able to find my sister and yours. I guess you haven't had any luck yet?"

I shook my head. "Nothing yet."

He didn't say anything else as Michael and I stepped out the back door. Through the glass in the window, I kept an eye on Grayson as he stood in the kitchen.

I glanced up at Michael, desperate for his wisdom and experience here. My emotions were too out of control to make any logical choices. "What do you think I should do? Should I ask for Grayson's help with this memory chip?"

Michael pressed his lips together, obviously burdened by the choice also. "It's a hard one, Elliot. I don't exactly know what to tell you. It's risky either way we look at it."

"Grayson is the only one who might be able to break into it," I said.

"He also has enough on the line that he could give this information away to save his sister. You may never know what's on that chip—and I know you don't want that."

"What are our other options?" I stared up at Michael. He was a smart man, and I trusted and valued his opinion. But there was no good solution here—only bad choices.

"We could ask Hunter," he suggested.

"Then we'll have to bring other people at the police department into this. It's not my first choice."

Michael sighed and looked off in the distance, rubbing his cheek. I could tell he was taking this seriously, as he should.

Suddenly, a light lit his eyes. "I have an idea. Let me run it past you and see what you think."

I braced myself for whatever he had to say.

And I prayed that it was a plan I might be able to live with.

CHAPTER THIRTY-THREE

AN HOUR LATER, everything had been set in motion.

And I hoped I didn't regret our choice.

Oscar had stopped by Grayson's sister's place, and we switched out cars, just in case anybody was looking for a familiar vehicle. Oscar told us to keep his car for as long as we needed.

Then Michael and I waited.

We'd given Grayson fake information—a list of made up names that should distract them for awhile until they realized the people there didn't really exist. Grayson had then called his contact and let him know that he had it. Now Grayson was supposed to meet this mysterious person to do the handoff.

While he did that, Michael and I were going to follow these men back to whatever location they were staying.

We prayed that when we did that, we'd find Ruth and Sarah.

There were so many ways this could go wrong.

I'd asked myself a million times if we needed to get the police involved. But if the police were involved, they might step in too soon. They might blow everything.

And I wasn't prepared for that to happen.

But we were running out of time. I couldn't take any chances. I had to get to my sister. She had to be rescued. Have her surgery. Be given a fresh start at life.

"Do you think our plan is going to work?" I turned toward Michael, wanting to see the truth in his eyes. What we were doing was risky. I hoped there was a payoff.

His gaze met mine. "I think this is the best plan we have considering all of our options."

"Do you think these guys are really going to believe the list we gave Grayson is the list they're looking for?"

"It seems like it's a good possibility," Michael said. "But all those pieces will fall in place."

I shook my head, trying to ward away any feelings of being overwhelmed. I needed to keep my head as clear as possible. I couldn't let my emotions win right now.

"I just can't believe everything that's happened," I finally said. "I can't believe that Grayson was lying to us. Can't believe there was nothing on that jump drive."

"When you're in this line of work, being covert means

everything. I'm sure your dad would have taught you a lot of lessons if he was still around. He seemed like he was a master at what he did."

"It does seem like that, doesn't it?"

"And you've got some of that in you." Michael offered an encouraging smile. "You're a natural at this job. It surprised even me."

I wasn't sure what I thought about that, so I nudged Michael's bicep with my knuckles. "You're always sweet-talking me."

He took my hand and kissed the top of my knuckles. "I mean it, Elliot. You're doing a great job. You've got a great sense of observation, you can tell when things are out of place faster than anybody I know, and you're a good judge of character as well. You've been a real asset to us at the office."

"Now you're just trying to make me blush."

Before we could say anything else, Grayson pulled out of the driveway.

Those men must have gotten back with him about a place to meet.

I exchanged a glance with Michael.

As the saying went, here went nothing.

MICHAEL and I stayed a safe distance behind Grayson as we followed him through town. He turned after Storm River and headed into a neighboring town. Once there, Grayson parked and climbed out. He glanced around before heading toward a gazebo in the center of the town square.

Michael and I had pulled behind several other cars parked on the side of the street. Thanks to Oscar's tinted windows, I didn't think anybody could see us inside. Just to be safe, I kept a lookout for anybody who might be watching.

I didn't see anyone suspicious.

Despite that, I still held my breath, still waited for something to go wrong.

But I prayed that wasn't the case.

Michael and I couldn't be seen. The last thing I wanted was to ruin this. It was essential that we remained behind the scenes if we wanted to follow these guys back to wherever they were going. Hopefully, these guys would lead us to Ruth and Sarah.

The nighttime both helped to conceal us and to conceal anyone who might be close. Thankfully, the town square itself was lit with old-fashioned streetlights.

As we waited, Michael reached over and rubbed my shoulder, as if he could sense my tension. "I know that waiting is the hard part."

"I just hope these guys fall for it." I watched as

Grayson stood awkwardly near the gazebo, waiting for these guys to show up.

I glanced at the time on my phone. These guys were supposed to be here any time now.

Hopefully, they'd show up soon.

As the minutes ticked by, my anxiety continued to grow.

Where were they? Too much time had passed. But we hadn't talked to Grayson. We hadn't confirmed anything.

I just needed to be patient.

But how long should I be patient? That was the question I wasn't sure about.

Finally, after thirty minutes had passed, Grayson glanced at his watch. He let out a sigh and glanced around.

He was beginning to think they weren't going to show up either, wasn't he?

This wasn't good.

Michael and I had staked everything on this plan.

So why weren't these guys who desperately wanted this information showing up?

Grayson remained at his spot. That was good. Maybe he wanted to wait this out a little bit longer.

Michael didn't say anything. He just settled down and waited.

I really hoped this paid off for us.

CHAPTER THIRTY-FOUR

FORTY MINUTES LATER, Grayson walked toward Oscar's car—and he didn't look happy.

Though I was afraid somebody was watching us, Grayson apparently did not have that same fear. He was giving our location away.

Michael lowered his window just a crack and hissed, "What are you doing?"

"They're onto us." Grayson leaned closer, his jaw flexing. "They're not coming."

I wanted to argue, but I couldn't. Whoever he was supposed to meet clearly wasn't going to show up.

"What do you think gave it away?" Michael asked. "We were careful."

"These guys have eyes and ears everywhere." Grayson shrugged and shook his head, looking tense enough to snap. "I don't know what happened, but this isn't going to work. We need to think of another plan."

"We don't have another plan." I rubbed my temples, that familiar headache reappearing. "Everything hinged on this."

Grayson let out another long breath. "Maybe we should just think this through tonight. Maybe in the morning, things will become more clear. But these guys are not coming tonight."

"They could be watching us now." I glanced around again, surprised that Grayson had even come up to us in public. "It's risky that you're even talking to us."

"They're not watching us." Grayson shook his head, leaving no room for doubt about what he thought.

"Why do you say that?" Michael asked.

"Because I've been standing there watching everybody come and go. These guys are not here, and they're not coming. Believe me."

Michael and I remained quiet a minute. There was nothing else to say. Our plan had failed. We were now back to square one.

"Let's reconvene in the morning and see if we can figure out something," Michael finally said. "I think you're right about tonight—there's nothing else we can do."

Grayson had one thing right. These guys definitely weren't going to show up now. And I wasn't sure what else we could do on the spur of the moment to make our plan happen.

We'd failed.

Again.

That word wouldn't leave my thoughts. Every time I turned around, I came face-to-face with the fact that I could have done better.

My dad would *not* be proud of me. He'd obviously expected more.

"Okay," Grayson said. "I can meet in the morning at the office. But we're running out of time."

He didn't have to tell me that. I couldn't forget.

I had fifteen hours until these men said they would kill my sister.

That meant there wasn't any time for sleep.

But it also meant I had no idea how to track down anybody in order to find my sister.

"MAYBE GRAYSON IS RIGHT," Michael said after his friend walked away. "Maybe the best thing we can do is to get some sleep. It's been a long day, and, I don't know about you, but my head is pounding."

"I can't even think about sleeping, not while knowing that Ruth is being held prisoner and that time is running out." I let my head fall back against the seat, hating the fact we'd hit another roadblock.

"But what else can we do tonight?" Michael asked. "Nothing."

I wasn't ready to give up yet. "We've got to think of another way to figure out what's on that memory chip. Maybe I can watch some online videos on it or something. We can figure it out."

The look Michael gave me made it clear my idea was horrible.

"I suppose not just anyone can figure out that kind of technology . . ." I finally conceded. "But my dad left it for me. He must have assumed that there was some way I could get into it."

"Now that could actually be a good point." Michael leaned back and looked off into the distance in thought. "Is there anything else he left you that we might be able to use this for?"

"I . . . I'm not sure."

He glanced at his watch. "Let's give ourselves another hour. Then we really do need to get some sleep. I know it's not what you want . . . but even an hour or two of rest might do us a world of good."

I agreed, and we went to the office.

Michael checked things out inside first. When he was certain it was safe, we hunkered down and locked the doors behind us. We couldn't risk any unexpected visitors.

As soon as I sank into my chair, Michael's phone rang. It was Chloe.

He talked to her for a few minutes and then she wanted to talk to me. Her cheerful voice brightened my day . . . and served as a grim reminder of what was at stake.

After Michael ended the call, I could feel his eyes on me. "What's going through your mind right now?"

A tear trickled down my cheek. "I don't know."

"Elliot . . ."

My gaze met his. "I feel like I've pulled you into the middle of a horrible situation."

"Elliot . . ." He grabbed my wrist and pulled me toward him.

I landed in his lap, and he wrapped his arms around me.

"It's okay not to be strong all the time," he murmured.

That seemed to be all I needed. The floodgates opened, and tears streamed from my eyes.

Michael didn't say anything. He just held me.

"I feel like I'm letting everyone down," I whispered, wiping my eyes with the edge of my shirt.

"You haven't let anyone down. You're fighting with everything in you to find answers."

"And I feel like I've gotten nowhere."

"But you have to know that's not true. You've made a ton of progress toward finding your sister. We just need a little more time."

"We don't have time." I shook my head. "And you have Chloe . . . if this doesn't end, what if they target her?"

"Chloe is fine, Elliot. We'll cross that bridge when we get there." He tightened his arms and kissed my temple.

I wasn't so sure about that.

I stood and reached for a tissue on my desk. As I did, my hand hit the photo of me and Ruth.

It fell to the ground and the picture frame broke into uncountable pieces.

"Look what I did now," I muttered.

But as I reached down to pick it up, something caught my eye.

Something I'd never seen on the frame before.

And possibly just what we were looking for.

CHAPTER THIRTY-FIVE

"WHAT IS THIS?" I held up the device that had been hidden in the frame.

The frame that my father had given me.

I'd just assumed he'd bought it at the store and that it was a run-of-the-mill decoration.

I'd been so wrong.

"May I?" Michael reached for it but didn't take it from my hands.

I placed it in his palm.

He held it up to the light and nodded slowly. "This is a jump drive. If I pop it open, I bet I'll find a place for that memory chip."

My father . . . he'd planned all of this, hadn't he? I'd always known he was brilliant. "Let's see what's on it then, shall we?"

"Let's."

Michael carefully took the memory chip and placed it in the device.

It fit perfectly.

I couldn't believe this jump drive had been hidden in front of me this whole time, and I'd never seen it. I was thankful we'd found it in the nick of time.

Michael inserted the device into his computer.

Then we waited to see what popped up on the screen.

The computer screen scrambled for a moment before various folders appeared.

This was it.

This was what we'd been looking for.

Michael glanced at me. "Shall we?"

I nodded and pointed to a folder reading, "The Bogota."

"What's the Bogota?"

"It was a huge building housing the poor in our capital city," I explained. "The government actually owned the building, but it collapsed about a year ago. Hundreds of people died."

"That's awful."

"It was really one of the catalysts for Xavier Flores taking over."

"What do you mean?" Michael asked.

"Leaders had allocated money to fix the building, but our former president vetoed it. Some people even said

President Acosta pocketed the money himself. People were furious and called him selfish. That's when the uprising really took root."

"That's terrible."

"It really was."

Michael paused for a moment before glancing at me. "You ready to see what's here?"

I swallowed hard. "I am."

―――――――

MY EYES WIDENED as I watched one of fifteen videos on the file.

They'd been taken on what was obviously a hidden camera.

And they showed Xavier Flores talking about how he'd framed Yerba's former President Acosta and made him look guilty for the Bogota's collapse.

He'd set up President Acosta to take the fall so he could rise to power.

I leaned back in my chair. "I can't believe this."

"If the people in Yerba found out about this there would be another uprising."

"You're right. There would be—especially if they saw this video. What's on the rest of them?"

Michael hit play. There was more of the same. More backroom deals being made between officials and the wealthy. They'd carefully planned their takedown of Acosta and didn't care who'd been killed in the process.

I sucked in a breath as a familiar face came on-screen.

Flores had met with Sergio.

I looked at the time stamp.

While we'd been dating.

He'd been a part of this. Had he only dated me to get close to my father?

It wouldn't surprise me.

"No wonder these people are desperate to get their hands on this," I muttered. "These recordings could bring down some very powerful people."

"Yes, they could."

And we'd only just started uncovering what was on that memory chip. What else was in these other digital folders?

CHAPTER THIRTY-SIX

"HOW ABOUT THAT FOLDER?" I pointed to another.

Michael clicked on it. A list of names appeared—there had to be at least thirty people listed. Most of the names appeared to be nicknames like Jay Bird and Walter Reed.

"Is this a list of bad guys?" Michael asked.

"I don't think so . . ." The truth pressed on me.

"What do you mean?"

I leaned back, letting my thoughts race and meander and wander. "I mean, these men already know who's profiting from the country's downfall. Plus, if I didn't have this list, they could just kill me and then their problem disappears. But they want this list for another reason."

"Because it's the opposite, isn't it?" Michael shook his head as realization rolled over his features. His voice climbed with excitement. "This must be a list of people who are capable of bringing the country down. These guys need to know who's on this list so they can do away with everyone and preserve what they've fought so hard to achieve—control of Yerba."

Our gazes met.

That had to be it. It was the only thing that made sense.

This was basically a hit list. The men who wanted to get their hands on this wanted all these people dead.

And when I said men, I wasn't 100 percent sure who I was talking about. I supposed Sergio was included. How about Mr. Harrington? Were they both behind this?

I stared at the names on the computer screen. Most of the names, I didn't recognize.

But my father had thought this information was valuable. He'd been killed for it. That was why someone was desperate to get their hands on it.

Whoever killed my father must have known there was a copy of the information in my possession. I wasn't sure how they knew. But it was the only reason they would come after me now.

As Michael scrolled down, we found a folder reading, "For Elliot."

Michael clicked on it.

Tears filled my eyes as I read his typed message to me.

My dearest Elliot,

If you're reading this, I'm most likely dead. And that means that you were smart enough to put all of this together. I knew you would be.

I'm sorry you're in the middle of things. I began collecting information more than a year ago. I had to have proof of what we were up against if we had any chance of winning. But our family has been under great threat as well.

I knew if I turned this information over that I'd be putting you all in danger. That was the last thing I wanted. But, if I'm dead, then you're in danger anyway.

That means, I need for you to finish the task I started.

Below, I've listed the names of people you should send these videos to. The truth must be known. I should have set things in motion myself. But maybe part of me was a coward who wanted to protect those I love over the greater good.

I love you girls more than anything, and every choice I've made has been because of you.

I'm sorry to leave this task in your hands, but I know you will do the right thing. You don't know it yet, but you are far more skilled than me in these matters. You have the abilities to put things together, to see inconsistencies, to separate yourself from your emotion. You're going to do great things one day, Elliot. I know you are.

I love you so much, and I'm so proud of you. Always know that.

Love,

Papa

More tears pressed at my eyes. Just when I thought there were none left to cry, more appeared.

"Your dad really believed in you," Michael said.

I nodded. "He did."

"What do you want to do?" His voice was prodding and soft.

I swallowed hard, knowing I didn't have a lot of time to think about this. It didn't matter anyway. I knew the right answer.

"I've got to send out this information," I said.

"If you're sure."

"I am."

Michael and I wasted no time sending the information to the people my dad had listed.

I also sent a copy of the videos to Michael and Hunter for safekeeping.

When we were done, I took the jump drive from my computer and stuffed it back into my pocket.

If my dad had barely been able to hide this, then what made me think that I could? And who could I trust with this information? The one person that I could think of was now dead.

Blaine.

If I had my guess, he was killed because someone knew he was on my father's side. His accident had not been an accident.

All of a sudden, I felt chilled.

I couldn't hand this information over.

But what was I supposed to do with it?

These men still had my sister. I had no doubt in my mind that they would kill her if I didn't give them what they wanted. But . . .

I glanced at my watch. I still had twelve hours to get them something. Chicken Man hadn't even given me instructions on how I was supposed to give the jump drive information to them.

Certainly, they would try to be in contact somehow or another.

Until then, I had to think, and I had to think fast.

IT WAS LATE. Past eleven o'clock, and I really needed to check on my mom. I should have checked on her sooner, but I'd been so distracted with everything going on.

I couldn't believe we were going on the end of Day Three of my sister being missing. It just seemed surreal.

I knew from when I talked to my mom earlier that the hospital transplant team had called more than once. My mom was trying to put them off, but now that the Amber

Alert had gone out, she couldn't keep the facts from them any longer. She'd been forced to tell them what was going on.

I waited to hear an update from her when I got home. Had they asked about the money? If we found Ruth —*when* we found her—how were we going to get the rest of the funds?

There were too many unknowns. Too many questions still.

Michael held my hand as we walked inside, almost as if he knew I needed the extra strength and support.

When I saw my mom, I noticed her eyes were watery with unshed tears.

I paused in the doorway. "Mama?"

She sprang from the couch and threw her arms around me. "Oh, Elliot. I'm so glad you're back."

"What's wrong? Did something happen?" Alarm raced through me.

I still had time. Those men shouldn't have done anything to Ruth yet. But since when were criminals upstanding citizens who kept their word? I knew the answer to that. They weren't.

"I got a call from the hospital," Mama started. "The team thinks they're going to have Ruth's new lungs as early as this weekend. But that means she'll need to get to the hospital to begin all of her presurgery prep and tests sooner. We have to find her

THE CRAFT OF BEING COVERT 247

or she's going to miss this opportunity . . . an opportunity to live."

My heart pounded against my chest. "We're going to find her, and we're going to have the money to make the surgery happen."

But even I could tell my words weren't as confident as they had once been.

Linda rose from the couch and gave Mom a hug before disappearing. She said she would be back in the morning if we needed her.

That left just the three of us.

A strange silence filled the air.

What did I say? Did I pour out everything I'd learned to my mom? There was no need to hold back on details anymore. She knew about my father. She knew about the jump drive.

All our secrets were out in the open now.

And it felt good. I wasn't going to lie.

"What did you learn today?" My mom took my arm and one of Michael's arms and led us to the couch. She waited until we were seated and then sat across from us.

I drew in a deep breath before I started into everything we'd learned. She listened carefully, nodding to let us know she understood.

When I finished, she burst into tears.

"How are we going to figure this out in only twelve hours?"

I reached into my pocket and pulled out the list that I'd printed. "I have the information they want. But if I give it to them, then the people on this list could end up dead."

"We can't let that happen either," my mom said. "Their blood will be on our hands."

"I know. I don't know what to do."

"Then I can make that decision for you," a new voice said. "Why don't you give me the list?"

I looked up as someone stepped into the room.

Someone wearing that familiar chicken costume and holding a gun.

My head began to spin.

How long had this man been in our house?

And the even bigger question . . . how much had he heard?

CHAPTER THIRTY-SEVEN

MY MOM GASPED beside me and drew back.

Michael rose to his feet and pushed himself in front of us.

"Who are you and what are you doing here?" he demanded.

I hardly heard his question. All I could think about was the fact that this man now knew that I had the list. But would he release Ruth if I gave it to him? And how could I even live with myself if I did that?

The questions all rushed at me. My head pounded as the weight of my choices pressed on my shoulders.

"I don't think you're in a good position to be asking questions right now," Chicken Man said. "I need that list."

I rose to my feet, feeling a surprising courage grip me. "And we need my sister."

"You'll get your sister when I get the list."

"How do I know that?" I asked.

"You're going to have to take my word for it."

"I'm going to need more than that," I said.

"Let's face it," Chicken Man said. "You do not have a lot of time to waste here. I know that your sister needs that surgery. Every moment is precious. So why do you not just hand over the list?"

My hands fisted at my sides. "And then what?"

"And then we will bring your sister back."

"Just like that?" I had a hard time believing that he was going to stay true to his word. Once he had what he wanted, what would his incentive be for keeping my sister alive? He obviously hadn't had enough incentive to keep my father living. I had no reason to think that he would change his mind now.

He stretched his hand out. "Give me the list."

I could tell the person behind the mask was trying to disguise his voice. Could it be Sergio? Mr. Harrington? One of those men I'd seen at Shipwrecks?

I really had no idea. Even now, part of me didn't even care.

There was too much on the line.

"Please," my mom said behind us. "Just give me my daughter back. Leave us alone. We have nothing to do with this."

"Then maybe your husband should not have involved

himself in matters that were none of his business." A new edge entered the man's voice.

I didn't think it was Sergio. What he was saying and the cadence of his words didn't match what I knew about Sergio. So who was it?

"My husband is dead, and we had nothing to do with his actions," Mama said. "It's bad enough that you killed him."

Chicken Man didn't say anything for a moment. "If he had just done what we had asked, we would not have had to do anything."

"How did you manage to disguise it as a heart attack?" Mama continued.

The man shrugged. "There are medications that can mimic that. It really was not that hard."

"You're despicable," I muttered.

Even though I suspected that my father had been killed, hearing the confirmation out loud made me sick to my stomach. I wanted to lunge across the room and throttle this man.

But it would be foolish.

Because I saw the gun in the man's hands. And I knew he would not hesitate to use it.

Which meant I had to think about my next choice very, very carefully.

I CLEARED MY THROAT, finally finding my voice again. "Why are you being such a coward? Why don't you show us who you are?"

"That is not important," the man said. "I need that list. And I want it now."

"I need proof. Proof that my sister will be returned to us alive and healthy."

He said nothing for a moment, and I was quite certain that he would change his mind.

But a moment later, he pulled his cell phone from a pocket and dialed. He muttered something into the mouthpiece before showing me the screen.

Ruth's image appeared on a live video.

My heart raced.

I stepped closer, desperately wanting to reach out to her. To talk to her.

But as I did, the man shoved his gun out farther. I knew if I got any closer, he would take drastic actions.

"Say something," the man demanded.

Tear-filled eyes looked at us from the screen.

"Mama," Ruth said. "Elliot. I'm okay."

But as soon as she said the words, a coughing fit seized her.

My heart pounded until an ache filled me. Ruth might be okay, but she wasn't okay. That was clear.

"That is enough," the man said.

Just as quickly as we'd seen her, the phone disappeared back into his pocket.

But this was far from being over.

"My father had a list of people who were on the opposite side of the uprising in Yerba." I tried to think things through and buy a little time. "You want that list of people so you can eliminate them. You see them as a threat."

"It does not matter. All that matters is that the list becomes mine."

"It's obviously important because you're willing to kill for it." My mind continued to race. "These people know things that could take down this entire new regime. It's the only reason why you would have put so much time and resources into this."

"Just give me the list." The man's voice sounded a little above a growl.

"You followed us to Storm River just so you could get that list. But my father wasn't stupid. He hid the information. He knew that you guys would be on his heels."

"Just give it to me," the man said.

"Which brings me to another point." More facts began to click together in my mind. "Why would you have killed Blaine Kingsley?"

The man said nothing.

"What kind of threat could he possibly be? He was only an ambassador."

I stared at Chicken Man. I could feel Michael and my mom standing on either side of me, waiting to see where I was going with this conversation.

That's when I knew I had to play my wild card.

"I guess there's an easy answer for that," I said. "Because the truth is that Blaine Kingsley didn't die. Am I right?"

I stared at him, waiting for his response.

The next thing I knew, he reached for his mask and pulled it off.

CHAPTER THIRTY-EIGHT

"BLAINE." My throat burned as the word escaped.

"It does not matter if you know who I am." He scowled as he stared at us. "This will all soon be over. And nobody is going to believe you."

"Because you're going to disappear with this list," I muttered. "You stand to make millions of dollars, don't you? You can disappear from the US and live off that money and no one will be the wiser. You and your cronies."

"All I want is the list," Blaine growled.

"My father trusted you. You were his friend. You were supposed to represent our country. How could you do this?"

"Things are complicated."

"You sold Yerba out for the sake of yourself," I continued, anger bubbling inside me. "Millions have lost their jobs and their homes and their livelihoods. How can you live with yourself?"

"Sometimes you just have to watch out for yourself."

"And that's the problem, isn't it? Too many people are watching out for themselves and not thinking about the bigger picture."

He let out a sigh. "Just give me that list, and I will be gone, Elliot."

"It's not going to work. You need to take me to my sister first."

"That is not going to happen."

"I thought you were dead," I muttered, trying to put the pieces together. "Who was the dead man in the car?"

"Someone else who betrayed us. No one you know."

I swallowed hard, realizing this man had no respect for the sanctity of life.

That only made this situation more dire.

I squared my shoulders, trying to sound tougher than I actually felt. "Unless you tell me where Ruth is, then I'm going to give the signal for the police to arrive. And when they do, you're going to be left out. All that money that you think you're getting, you're not going to see a dime of it."

His eyes narrowed. "You do not know what you are talking about."

I pointed to a lamp in the corner, as well as a fake

plant on the opposite side of the room. "You're not the only one who is capable of setting up cameras. All of this is on video. You will be going down. Now I need you to make a phone call and have your men bring my sister here."

He let out a chuckle. "You think you are so clever, do you not?"

I fisted my hands at my side. "I don't want to be clever. I just want my sister. Now make the phone call."

He stared at me another moment before pulling out his phone. Just as he did before, he dialed a number and mumbled something into the mouthpiece. A few minutes later, he slipped the phone back into his pocket. "Done. But when she gets here, I want a trade-off."

"You don't deserve that information," I told him.

"I have to admit that you are a more clever opponent than I thought you would be." Blaine's voice hardened. "But it is time to stop playing this game."

I'd love to stop playing this game. He'd get no argument from me there. "How long until Ruth gets here?"

"Ten minutes."

That meant that she hadn't been very far away. Only ten minutes. My mind raced as I tried to think about where she might have been held.

I didn't think I was going to be able to wait those ten minutes, though.

I'd sent Hunter this information. I had no doubt he'd be showing up here soon.

When I'd begun to think things through, Blaine had been the only one who made sense as far as being behind this.

His death seemed so out of the blue. According to Hunter, his body had been burned beyond recognition and the skid marks at the scene were suspicious.

What I still wasn't sure about was if Sergio was actually involved in this or not. But based on the fact that he had met with Grayson, I was inclined to think that he was.

Now I just needed to use some time until my sister got here.

I couldn't forget the fact that Blaine was the one who had the gun right now.

I prayed he didn't realize my bluff when I said that there were cameras hidden in this house.

"Blaine, how could you do this?" My mom stared at him, fire igniting in her gaze. "My husband trusted you."

"And I regret the people that I have let down." He shrugged. "However, this is how life works sometimes."

"You're despicable," Mama muttered.

"You only know half of it," I said. "Flores killed all those people in the Bogota. Then he helped frame President Acosta for it, all so he could have power and money."

Mama gasped. "No . . ."

"You have no proof."

I smiled at him.

His eyes widened.

He hadn't known about the videos, had he? He only thought there was a list.

"I am sorry." Blaine shifted. "But I cannot play this game anymore."

With that, he raised his gun.

I knew he wasn't about to hold up to his end of the bargain.

"ELLIOT!" I heard Michael shout.

The next instant, I hit the floor. Michael's body covered mine.

Just as that happened, someone rushed in through the front door.

The police.

With their guns drawn.

I looked up just in time to see everything register on Blaine's face. The next instant, he raised his gun higher.

But it wasn't pointed at me.

Blaine pointed it at himself.

Certainly, he knew what was at stake. If he was discovered, he would be a man without a country. And without any money to make a way for himself.

A blast filled the air, and I squeezed my eyes shut.

I knew what had happened.

Blaine had shot himself.

More shots sounded from around me.

Michael murmured comforting words in my ear, but I barely heard them.

My mom screamed, followed by a cry.

Michael eased to the side as I pushed myself up, almost incognizant of anything happening around me. I crawled across the floor until I reached my mom. Then I threw my arms around her. We collapsed into each other's embrace.

Michael appeared beside us, offering support.

Then Hunter came into view. The deep frown on his face was nothing short of apologetic. He knew the stakes.

He knew that the one person who knew where my sister was being held was now dead.

How were we going to find Ruth?

CHAPTER THIRTY-NINE

MICHAEL HELD the water bottle up to me again. "You need to drink something. You're not going to be any good to anyone if you pass out."

My head throbbed. How were we ever going to find Ruth now?

The question almost made me feel hollow inside.

Because the answer seemed impossible. The time limit had passed. The person who was supposedly coming with Ruth hadn't come.

Which meant we were at a dead end.

"I'm sorry, Elliot." Hunter stopped beside me. "I didn't have a chance to talk him out of shooting himself."

I nodded, knowing his words were true. But I desperately wished there had been another way.

"What do we do now?" My mom looked up with red-rimmed eyes. "We have to find her."

"We're going to try and trace calls to his cell phone over the past couple of days," Hunter said. "Maybe that could lead us to her location. We're using all the resources at our disposal to locate Sergio and make sure he doesn't leave the country. My guess is that he may know where Ruth might be."

"He doesn't want to get caught," I said. "He's probably on his way back to Yerba by now."

"We can't give into despair." Michael's voice left no room for argument. "Let's think this through. Blaine said Ruth was only ten minutes away."

"If he was telling the truth," I reminded him.

"Grayson also remembered that, when he was held, he kept thinking he smelled fresh doughnuts."

"But we checked all of the local doughnut shops that were nearby," I reminded him. "There was nothing at any of them that would indicate where she might be."

"Maybe we need to look outside our initial parameters," Michael said. "Maybe it's not an exclusive doughnut shop. Maybe it's a shop that also sells doughnuts."

For the first time since this mess had started, I felt a spark of hope in me. Maybe Michael was onto something. "How do we even narrow that down?"

"We can do another online search," Hunter said. "That would be a good place to start. Especially if you think it's in a ten-minute perimeter of this house. That will help us narrow it down even further."

"Let's do it." I sat up. "It's better than nothing. If Ruth is going to make her transplant date, she's got to get to the hospital tomorrow to begin her pretreatment."

"I'm sorry all this is happening." Hunter paused beside me. "I really am."

I nodded, trying to silently communicate that I wasn't holding him responsible. I just hated the way that things had escalated.

Just then, I sat up even straighter.

There was one place I could think of nearby that could sell a small selection of doughnuts. A place that had also thrown away a lot of fresh fruit scraps. Tropical food scraps.

Velma had seen them in the dumpster behind the building.

How could I not have realized this earlier?

I stood. "I think I might know where Ruth is."

I STOOD on the sidewalk near the Driscoll and Associates office.

A group of police officers were searching the rooms above the bakery right down the street.

I wasn't sure how I had missed this fact. Maybe I had

gotten so used to the smell of baked goods outside the office that it hadn't even registered with me that this could be the location.

But what better place to keep an eye on us than by renting the apartment above the bakery? That would give these men a bird's eye view of when I came and went from the office.

Michael kept one arm around me and one around my mom as we waited there.

Yes, my mom had left the house. There was no way we were going to be able to hold her back from seeing the outcome of this.

Even though I knew that time hadn't slowed, it almost felt like it had as I waited for the results.

We should find out soon whether or not Ruth was inside. Grayson's sister also.

Michael had called him, and the man was on his way here now.

I could hardly breathe as I waited.

Please, God, let her be inside. Let her be okay. Grayson's sister too.

A moment later, men emerged from a door at the front of the building.

Joy filled me when I saw Ruth being led out with a blanket over her shoulders.

Mama and I took off in a run toward her.

My sister was okay.

She was really okay.

CHAPTER FORTY

MAMA and I threw our arms around Ruth as tears rushed down our faces.

Ruth hugged us back equally as hard.

Despite the circumstances, she didn't seem any worse for the experience. I was so grateful for that.

Ruth pulled back and wiped the tears from beneath her eyes. "I knew you would find me."

"We haven't stopped looking," I told her. "And we weren't going to."

I glanced behind her and saw another woman being led down the steps. As she reached the sidewalk, a red sports car pulled up in front of the building. Grayson hopped out and ran toward her.

That had to be his sister, Sarah.

Thankfully, it looked like we would all be getting a happy ending.

I was grateful because I knew things could have turned out so much differently.

"What happened?" I turned back to Ruth.

She wiped beneath her eyes again, obviously emotional. "I was walking home when this car pulled up beside me. The man behind the wheel asked for directions, and, the next thing I knew, he sprayed something in my face. Everything went black. When I woke up, I was in a room above the bakery."

"They didn't hurt you, did they?" Mama narrowed her eyes as she studied Ruth.

Ruth shook her head. "No, they kept me fed. But those men . . . they were from Yerba."

"Did you see Sergio?" I asked.

"Sergio?" Ruth shook her head, confusion crossing her gaze. "No, why?"

"Just wondering. It doesn't matter right now. All that matters is that you're okay."

Two paramedics stepped toward her, waiting patiently for their chance to check her out. Mama and I stepped back so Ruth could sit on a gurney.

"You are just like your father," my mom muttered to me. "I think I've always known that. I just didn't want to acknowledge it."

"Maybe that's why you kept encouraging me to work behind the scenes instead?"

Mama nodded. "I couldn't stand thinking about two people I love being in this line of work. At the same time, who am I to keep you from doing what you love?"

"PI work is a little bit different than being a spy," I told her.

"Maybe, but the danger could be the same."

I couldn't argue with that. Instead, I asked, "What do you think will happen with Yerba?"

She shook her head. "I don't know. Now that they have this information, people will begin to put pressure on Flores. We can only hope that means he will resign from office."

That would be the best-case scenario. But I had some doubts as to whether or not that would work.

As Michael joined us, I excused myself.

I had one more question for Ruth. It wasn't totally important. I probably shouldn't even ask it now. But I wanted to know.

As a paramedic stepped away, I crept closer and lowered my voice. "Ruth, who is MamasBoy, and why were you talking to him online?"

Her face fell. As the paramedic appeared again to take her blood pressure, she shook her head. "I don't know what I was thinking. He just seemed older and interesting and..."

"And what?"

Her gaze pulled up to meet mine. "Sometimes it just feels like I'm not going to have the opportunity to experience the things in life that other people have, like falling in love. I thought that maybe if I met him, that I could maybe just get a taste of romance and what it's like to feel important."

I squeezed her hand. "You are important, Ruth."

She shrugged. "I know. It was dumb. Stupid. If I could do it again, I wouldn't have ever connected with him."

"Why him of all people? Aren't there kids at your school? Guys closer to your own age?"

She shrugged. "I find boys my age to be so immature. I thought an older man might be the answer, but I was wrong."

"What did you do with him?" And I held my breath as I waited to hear her answer. Part of me didn't want to know.

"He just gave me rides a couple of times. That's it. I promise."

"He didn't try anything else?" I studied her face, determined to see whether or not she was telling the truth.

She shook her head. "No. He was kind of creepy, but he was pretty nice too. He didn't know I was a high schooler."

I could tell by her picture that Marcus may have been deceived.

I remembered that message I'd read, the one she'd sent to her friend that mentioned how sad she'd felt lately. "Ruth . . . were you really that unhappy?"

Again, it was a bad time. But I had to know. I had to put my questions to rest.

"I just miss Dad. And Yerba. And I know how much pressure this surgery has been putting on you and Mama. It's been a lot, and I wish I didn't have to put you in that position."

"We would do anything for you," I reminded her.

She nodded. "I know."

"We need to take her to the hospital to begin her prep for the double lung transplant," one of the paramedics said.

Ruth's eyes widened. "What?"

I nodded in affirmation. "It's true. You're next on the list. But you need to get to the hospital."

"I can't believe this." Her hand went over her mouth as if covering it in surprise.

I motioned to Mama. I could ride with Michael to the hospital. But Mama would want to be with Ruth.

My mom climbed in the back of the ambulance with my sister. Before she did, she exchanged a look with me.

I knew exactly what it meant.

Ruth was going to the hospital, but we still hadn't procured the funds we needed.

What were we going to do?

"I love you, Ruth," I called.

"I love you too!"

The worst of this was over. Now I just needed to pray that Ruth's surgery was successful—and that we found the money for it.

———

AS MICHAEL and I waited to give our statements, I heard a footstep behind me.

I turned around and saw . . . Mr. Harrington appear.

I stepped back, bracing myself for another confrontation. Did I need to call for the police?

I glanced behind me.

They were all preoccupied with the building where Ruth and Sarah had been kept.

"Elliot." Mr. Harrington's voice sounded grim and serious. "Michael."

I crossed my arms, waiting to hear why he'd risked coming out here now to talk to me. He had to have a good reason. "What are you doing here at this hour?"

"I've been keeping an eye on you."

Andrea Marino stepped out behind him. "Me too."

What was going on here? Certainly these two knew that all I had to do was yell, and help would appear.

"What are you both talking about?" Michael scooted

closer to me, his muscles hard and his jaw flexed. "What are you doing here?"

"We knew your father, Elliot," Harrington explained. "We're working together to bring down this new regime."

Wait . . . was he trying to say that he was one of the good guys? I wasn't sure I was ready to buy that. His name hadn't been on the list. Then again, they'd mostly been nicknames.

"You're from Yerba?" Harrington just didn't seem South American.

He nodded. "I left when I was only a toddler, but my brother stayed behind with my mother. He's still there, unable to leave right now."

I suppose it made sense now that I knew he had a personal stake in this.

"And my husband worked with your dad while they were in the field," Andrea said. "My husband wanted Lily to befriend Ruth so we could keep an eye on your family —so we could help keep you safe."

"But what about the bigger house you've been looking at?"

She let out a laugh. "Lily must have told you about that. We've been looking because we may need to move, out of necessity. Being married to a former spy is . . . well, it has its challenges, to say the least."

I believed both of them. Maybe I shouldn't, but there

were no signs they were lying. "Why are you here tonight?"

"We know you found the information your father left," Harrington said.

"And I sent it to the people he asked me to send it to —including the media. Word should be leaking about what happened there. I expect there to be backlash toward Flores."

Harrington nodded. "I expect the same. You did good work. Your father would be proud."

My cheeks warmed. "Thank you."

"I also have this for you." He handed me an envelope.

I stared at it a moment before tugging at the seal. When I'd ripped through the top, I pulled out a piece of paper inside. My eyes widened when I realized what it was. "A check?"

"I was the one who promised a cash reward to the person offering information leading to the arrest of the Beltway Killer. You're that person."

"I thought the reward money was stalled under bureaucratic red tape," I said. "That's what Hunter told me."

"I apologize for the delay," Harrington said. "There were some things we had to take care of first."

Michael's arm slipped around me as tears pricked my eyes.

I glanced up at him. "We have money for my sister's surgery."

He smiled. "That's great news."

"But this isn't all mine—" I hadn't found that killer alone.

Michael raised his hand. "Keep it. No one on our team is going to argue with you about that."

"You don't think?"

He nodded. "I don't. That's a true fact."

Warmth filled my chest.

Maybe everything really was falling in place.

CHAPTER FORTY-ONE

THREE DAYS LATER, my sister was having her double lung transplant.

Michael and I sat with Mama in the hospital waiting room, anxious for the results. The surgery itself would take between eight and twelve hours, so we would be here for a while.

The past few days had been a blur.

Sergio had been arrested before he could leave the country. He was being investigated on possible kidnapping charges. Several other arrests had also been made.

More of my father's friends had come forward to verify the information that I'd sent out.

And the best news: Flores was now out of power in Yerba.

It turned out that a high-ranking military leader from

Yerba had a brother who died when that building collapsed. When he heard what Flores had done, he commanded his men to take action against Flores.

Flores was now in a Yerbian prison, and President Acosta was back in power.

I didn't see myself going back to Yerba. Not really. But it would be nice to have that option someday. It would be nice to be able to take Michael there, to show him where I'd grown up. To pick him a fresh papaya so he could know what it tasted like.

I looked up as somebody else entered the waiting area.

It was Hunter . . . and Kitty Kight.

Kitty Kight? What were the two of them doing together?

Based on the look that Hunter gave Kitty, it appeared the two of them might be an item.

Was it possible?

I wasn't sure, but this wasn't the time to ask.

They sat across from us.

"Any updates?" Hunter asked.

"Last we heard, Ruth is doing fine," I said. "Now it's just a waiting game."

"We thought that maybe you could use some company," Kitty explained.

"We appreciate it," I said. "Thank you."

"What are the updates on Blaine?" Mama asked.

He was on life support at a different hospital.

"We're still waiting for the doctor's final word on his condition," Hunter said. "It's too early to say."

"Part of me wants to see him pay for what he did," Mama said. "I want him to answer questions, to face consequences. Death seems too easy."

"I agree," Hunter said.

A couple more people stepped into the room just then. Oscar and Velma. We welcomed them into our little corner of the waiting area.

I watched as Hunter and Oscar assessed each other for a moment. Their silent standoff ended with a subtle nod from both of them. Whatever beef they had between them must have been settled.

I waited until Hunter and Kitty left a few minutes later to ask Oscar about it.

"Whatever happened between the two of you?" I asked.

"It's all water under the bridge," Oscar said. "But when I was a detective on the squad, Hunter had just started as a patrol officer. I got involved with someone I was working a case on, and Hunter reported me. He did the right thing. It's just taken me a long time to admit it."

None of what Oscar said surprised me. I could totally see it playing out.

But what did that mean for Michael and me?

The two of us exchanged a glance. Did we need to come clean to Oscar about our relationship status?

"I know that you're dating," Oscar stated with a little roll of his eyes.

My eyes widened. "Why would you say that?"

"It's obvious, and it has been for a while."

I shifted, suddenly feeling uncomfortable. "What does this mean for my future with Driscoll and Associates?"

"I'm glad you asked because I've been thinking about some changes."

"What kind of changes?" I held my breath. The last thing I wanted was to get Michael fired. He had a daughter to take care of.

"The name of my company has been Driscoll and Associates for a long time. But I've never truly had any associates. And I also know that you guys are invaluable to me. How would you two feel about coming on as my associates?"

"Really?" The word nearly squealed out of my mouth.

"Don't jump too far ahead." Oscar raised his hand. "You're going to have to go ahead and get your PI license just like we've planned. But I think the three of us could make a good team." Oscar glanced at Velma. "The four of us."

Velma shrugged and smiled. "I don't want to be a PI. Believe me, I'm happy working the front desk."

"And you do a great job holding us all together," I told her.

"Thanks. You guys give me a lot to work with."

The four of us let out a little chuckle.

Oscar and Velma stayed another hour, and then they left, and we settled back for the long wait to the end of the surgery. I was thankful to have so many people on my side. When I'd first moved here, I hadn't seen that happening. I'd felt so alone.

But things had turned around.

One of the nurses appeared every few hours to let us know how things were going.

So far so good.

"I think I'm going to stretch my legs and get a little coffee," I said.

Michael stood beside me. "Do you mind if I join you?"

"That sounds great."

Linda was here with my mom, so I knew she wouldn't be alone.

As we stepped out into the hallway, Michael took my hand in his. The circumstances in our lives lately had bonded us. That was certain. I couldn't help but think that the two of us were meant for each other. I'd never felt like this with someone before.

As we rounded the corner, we nearly collided with someone.

"Daddy! Daddy! Daddy!" Seven-year-old Chloe nearly flew into her father's arms.

Michael wrapped his arms around her and swung her up. "How's my little girl doing?"

"I'm good, Daddy. But I missed you."

Beyond Chloe, I spotted Michael's parents walking toward us.

I hadn't met them before, but they were pastors for a large mega church. I had to admit, I was nervous about being introduced, and I had never seen it happening like this.

They stopped in front of us.

"We thought you might want to see Chloe today," Michael's mom said. "Children always make our days a little brighter, don't they?"

"Yes, they do."

Michael lowered Chloe to the floor before looking at me. "Mom, Dad, this is Elliot. Elliot this is my mom and dad."

They both nodded and extended their hands.

"We've heard a lot about you," Michael's mom said.

"Lots of good things," his dad added. "It's our pleasure to meet you."

"The pleasure is mine," I told them. "Thank you for bringing Chloe by for us."

"We're happy to hear that your sister is finally getting the surgery," Michael's dad said. "Any updates?"

I told him the latest.

"We'd love to sit with you and pray over her surgery," he continued. "If you wouldn't mind."

"That would be great." I would never say no to prayer.

"Why don't you guys meet us in the waiting room?" Michael said. "Elliot and I are going to get some coffee but will be there in just one minute."

"Sounds good." Michael's mom flashed me another subdued smile.

As soon as they disappeared down the hall, I turned to Michael. "They seem nice."

"They are. I couldn't ask for better grandparents for Chloe."

"I'm glad they could come. It's very sweet of them."

Something shifted in Michael. His muscles seemed to tense as he rubbed his lips together and faced me. I sensed he was about to say something important.

"There's something I've been meaning to tell you, Elliot." His voice dropped down lower.

My heart thumped in my chest when I heard how serious he sounded. "What's that?"

"I know it's probably too soon." He pushed a hair behind my ear, his gaze glimmering with emotion. "But I love you, Elliot Ransom."

Something burst inside my heart as I heard his words. His proclamation felt like a soothing balm to my battered heart. "I don't think it's too soon to say that at all."

He raised an eyebrow and continued to stare into my eyes. "You don't?"

"No, because I have been thinking the same thing about you. I love you too, Michael Straley."

A grin stretched across his face. "I am so glad to hear that."

Our gazes caught, and everything around me froze.

Michael slowly leaned toward me. His arms slipped around my waist, and he tugged me close enough that I pressed up against his hard chest.

As my arms looped around his neck, our lips met. The action seemed so full of promise, of hope.

A few minutes later, we had our coffee in hand as we went back to the waiting room. As soon as we stepped inside, the doctor came into the room to give us an update.

I held my breath as I waited to hear what he had to say.

The balding, fifty-something man turned to address us. "I'm happy to tell you that Ruth has come through the surgery just fine. She's in recovery now, but you should be able to see her within the next couple of hours—one visitor at a time, of course. I think she's really going to enjoy this new set of lungs."

Michael threw his arms around me then my mother in a moment of victory. As we stood there embracing each other, Chloe joined us also. I pulled her into our circle, happy—thrilled—to have her as a part of it.

My mom pulled back and wiped the tears of joy from beneath her eyes. "Maybe I can actually get some sleep at night now."

"Praise God!" Michael's dad said. "I'm so glad things went well."

I sagged against Michael as my worries dissipated—at least, for a moment.

I still had a lot to learn about the art of being a sleuth and the finer practices of being covert. But I looked forward to every second of learning more . . . in honor of my dad.

And with Michael by my side, my future seemed brighter. I couldn't wait for Chloe to be a part of my life. I looked forward to being a more integral part of Driscoll and Associates. And I prayed that things continued to turn around in Yerba.

I squeezed Michael's hand.

What a trek through the jungle in mudslide season it had been so far. That was Yerbian for, as Michael might say, what a ride.

What a ride.

Just then, something swooped by my head. I ducked and looked up as a bird flew toward the fake tree in the corner.

"What?" I muttered, watching the little finch as he

landed on a branch and glanced around the waiting room.

"It must have come in from outside." My mom followed my gaze. "Those automatic doors make it easy."

Michael leaned closer and whispered, "Birds aren't real."

"What?" I remembered the T-shirts he loved to wear with his conspiracy theories on them. I thought they were just a joke . . .

"If it flies, it spies." Michael flashed a smile.

I let out a groan. "Please, tell me you're not serious."

"In light of everything that's happened . . ." He shrugged, leaving me hanging as to what his true thoughts were.

I glanced at the bird again and squeezed my eyes shut.

Was I actually considering the possibility that birds were government-controlled drones? I'd been caught up in the world of espionage for too long now.

"Be careful what you say," Michael whispered, still staring at the bird. "They're listening . . ."

"You're so funny."

Michael cocked his eyebrow. "But am I?"

I took a step back. "Let me go call a maintenance worker."

I needed this bird out of here . . . now.

YOU MIGHT ALSO ENJOY ...
THE SQUEAKY CLEAN MYSTERY SERIES

On her way to completing a degree in forensic science, Gabby St. Claire drops out of school and starts her own crime-scene cleaning business. When a routine cleaning job uncovers a murder weapon the police overlooked, she realizes that the wrong person is in jail. She also realizes that crime scene cleaning might be the perfect career for utilizing her investigative skills.

#1 Hazardous Duty

#2 Suspicious Minds

#2.5 It Came Upon a Midnight Crime (novella)

#3 Organized Grime

#4 Dirty Deeds

#5 The Scum of All Fears

#6 To Love, Honor and Perish

COMPLETE BOOK LIST

Squeaky Clean Mysteries:

#1 Hazardous Duty

#2 Suspicious Minds

#2.5 It Came Upon a Midnight Crime (novella)

#3 Organized Grime

#4 Dirty Deeds

#5 The Scum of All Fears

#6 To Love, Honor and Perish

#7 Mucky Streak

#8 Foul Play

#9 Broom & Gloom

#10 Dust and Obey

#11 Thrill Squeaker

#11.5 Swept Away (novella)

#12 Cunning Attractions

#13 Cold Case: Clean Getaway

#14 Cold Case: Clean Sweep

#15 Cold Case: Clean Break

#16 Cleans to an End (coming soon)

While You Were Sweeping, A Riley Thomas Spinoff

The Sierra Files:

#1 Pounced

#2 Hunted

#3 Pranced

#4 Rattled

The Gabby St. Claire Diaries (a Tween Mystery series):

The Curtain Call Caper

The Disappearing Dog Dilemma

The Bungled Bike Burglaries

The Worst Detective Ever

#1 Ready to Fumble

#2 Reign of Error

#3 Safety in Blunders

#4 Join the Flub

#5 Blooper Freak

#6 Flaw Abiding Citizen

#7 Gaffe Out Loud

#8 Joke and Dagger

#9 Wreck the Halls

#10 Glitch and Famous (coming soon)

Raven Remington
   Relentless 1
   Relentless 2 (coming soon)

Holly Anna Paladin Mysteries:
   #1 Random Acts of Murder
   #2 Random Acts of Deceit
   #2.5 Random Acts of Scrooge
   #3 Random Acts of Malice
   #4 Random Acts of Greed
   #5 Random Acts of Fraud
   #6 Random Acts of Outrage
   #7 Random Acts of Iniquity

Lantern Beach Mysteries
   #1 Hidden Currents
   #2 Flood Watch
   #3 Storm Surge
   #4 Dangerous Waters
   #5 Perilous Riptide
   #6 Deadly Undertow

Lantern Beach Romantic Suspense
   Tides of Deception
   Shadow of Intrigue

Storm of Doubt

Winds of Danger

Rains of Remorse

Lantern Beach P.D.

On the Lookout

Attempt to Locate

First Degree Murder

Dead on Arrival

Plan of Action

Lantern Beach Escape

Afterglow (a novelette)

Lantern Beach Blackout

Dark Water

Safe Harbor

Ripple Effect

Rising Tide

Crime á la Mode

Deadman's Float

Milkshake Up

Bomb Pop Threat

Banana Split Personalities

The Sidekick's Survival Guide

The Art of Eavesdropping

The Perks of Meddling

The Exercise of Interfering

The Practice of Prying

The Skill of Snooping

The Craft of Being Covert

Carolina Moon Series

Home Before Dark

Gone By Dark

Wait Until Dark

Light the Dark

Taken By Dark

Suburban Sleuth Mysteries:

Death of the Couch Potato's Wife

Fog Lake Suspense:

Edge of Peril

Margin of Error

Brink of Danger

Line of Duty

Cape Thomas Series:

Dubiosity

Disillusioned

Distorted

Standalone Romantic Mystery:
> The Good Girl

Suspense:
> Imperfect
> The Wrecking

Sweet Christmas Novella:
> Home to Chestnut Grove

Standalone Romantic-Suspense:
> Keeping Guard
> The Last Target
> Race Against Time
> Ricochet
> Key Witness
> Lifeline
> High-Stakes Holiday Reunion
> Desperate Measures
> Hidden Agenda
> Mountain Hideaway
> Dark Harbor
> Shadow of Suspicion
> The Baby Assignment
> The Cradle Conspiracy
> Trained to Defend

Nonfiction:

Characters in the Kitchen

Changed: True Stories of Finding God through Christian Music (out of print)

The Novel in Me: The Beginner's Guide to Writing and Publishing a Novel (out of print)

ABOUT THE AUTHOR

USA Today has called Christy Barritt's books "scary, funny, passionate, and quirky."

Christy writes both mystery and romantic suspense novels that are clean with underlying messages of faith. Her books have won the Daphne du Maurier Award for Excellence in Suspense and Mystery, have been twice nominated for the Romantic Times Reviewers' Choice Award, and have finaled for both a Carol Award and Foreword Magazine's Book of the Year.

She is married to her Prince Charming, a man who thinks she's hilarious—but only when she's not trying to be. Christy is a self-proclaimed klutz, an avid music lover who's known for spontaneously bursting into song, and a road trip aficionado.

When she's not working or spending time with her family, she enjoys singing, playing the guitar, and exploring small, unsuspecting towns where people have no idea how accident-prone she is.

Find Christy online at:
www.christybarritt.com
www.facebook.com/christybarritt
www.twitter.com/cbarritt

Sign up for Christy's newsletter to get information on all of her latest releases here: www.christybarritt.com/newsletter-sign-up/

If you enjoyed this book, please consider leaving a review.

Made in the USA
Middletown, DE
03 May 2024

53801613R00179